Seth's Doll

A CLUB ALIAS NOVEL

KD ROBICHAUX

Featured Song:

Lick by Joi featuring Sleepy Brown

Written by Joi, Sleepy Brown, Rico Wade, Ray Murray & Brandon Bennett.

Also by KD Robichaux

All links available at www.kdrobichaux.com

THE BLOGGER DIARIES TRILOGY:

Wished for You

Wish He Was You

Wish Come True

THE CLUB ALIAS SERIES:

Confession Duet (Before the Lie & Truth Revealed)

Seven: A Club Alias Novel

Mission: Accomplished (Knight Novella Boxed Set)

Knight: A Club Alias Novel

Doc: A Club Alias Novel

Astrid: A Club Alias Short Story

Seth's Doll: A Club Alias Novel

CLUB ALIAS MEMBERS SERIES:

Scary Hot: A Club Alias/Until Series Crossover

Moravian Rhapsody: A Club Alias Novella

A Lesson in Blackmail

XOXO

Plant Daddy Part 1

Plant Daddy Part 2

THE SUBMISSIVE DIARIES (a CLUB ALIAS SPINOFF SERIES):

Plant Daddy (Boxed Set of Part 1 and 2)

THE ADVENTURE CHANNEL SERIES

No Trespassing

Dishing Up Love

COWRITTEN WITH CC MONROE

Steal You

Number Neighbor

To Have and to Hold

Bad Medicine

PUBLISHED IN AURORA ROSE REYNOLDS'S

HAPPILY EVER ALPHA WORLD:

Until We Meet Again

Scary Hot

Until Cece

Foreword

A note from the author:

This story features a new character in the Club Alias world, Crystal Garcia. If you've read other books in this series, you might remember a couple of side characters with that first name. That's because one of my very best friends in the book world (and in life) is Crystal Burnette.

Real-life Crystal is genuinely one of the greatest humans in existence. She is sweet, loving, truly soul-deep kind, and 100% a good girl. Crystal also happens to be black.

When we became friends all those years ago, I made her a promise that whenever I wrote a not-so-good girl, I'd name the character after her; that way she could live vicariously through my fictional baddies. Among other things, she's been a sex-trafficking prostitute–which made her laugh until she had tears in her eyes—and now, in this story, she gets to be a retired Vegas showgirl who owns a pole-dancing workout studio.

After I wrote the first chapter and sent it to her, something *then* occurred to me, so I had to call her and freaked out a little.

"Oh, God, Crystal. I just realized I wrote a black stripper. I wrote a stripper… who is a *black* woman. I wasn't even thinking. I was just writing my friend into a bad bitch like I always do, and it didn't even occur to me that *that* could be taken badly, since I'm a white author. I didn't have to worry about the prostitute in Doc, since I made her catty white bitch! Do I need to change what this Crystal looks like?"

After telling me to breathe, she told me, "Kayla, I love you. Like, seriously. I love you for even just *being* worried about it. Now, yes, there could be readers who get mad that you've made your stripper character black, because they'll think it's a stereotype of 'black woman using her body to make ends meet' kind of thing. But guess what. There *are* black strippers. And from what I've read so far, she isn't the stereotypical 'black girl who dances to make enough money to raise the kids she's got at home.' Plus, don't you dare allow someone to take away my opportunity to be an exotic dancer! And one who *looks* like me! It's my time to shine, dammit!"

So, in conclusion, don't come after me. My good-girl bestie Crystal wanted to be a bad-bitch, black stripper, and good girls get rewarded in my world. So, a bad-bitch, black stripper, Crystal shall be.

Love,

An ally making a conscious effort to do her part and trying her best

Dedication

For the timid ones with the freak inside who just want him to take control and tell you, "Open up like my good little slut," and then push you 'til it hurts just right…

This one's for you, my beautiful little bookwhore.

CHAPTER 1

Twyla

"THE SHIPMENT of new dildos and intimacy companions were delivered this morning, boss. Just in time for the big sale. I left them all in the boxes for you, since I know you prefer to inspect the ones we've never carried before," Christi tells me, grabbing her purse from the safe beneath the register. She tosses it on her shoulder, then rounds the counter, giving me a high-five when I hold my hand up as she passes me on her way to the front door.

I ignore the little bit of panic that hits me when she reminds me how close we are to our bi-annual sale, which this year happens to land on my husband's birthday. And I haven't figured out a worthy enough present to get for him.

"Awesome. I've been dying to see for myself just how 'life-like' these things actually feel," I reply, pushing my glasses up my nose as I turn my head toward the back room, but her giggle has me facing her once again, my eyes narrowing. "What?"

She smirks and shrugs. "Nothing, Twy. Just didn't think you swung that way."

My brow furrows, my confusion written all over my face—as usual. "Huh?"

Christi rolls her eyes then says, "The sex dolls. They're all… you know… female."

My face flushes as it always does when a misunderstanding like this happens, no matter how long I've worked here at Toys for Twats. Even after I took over as the head honcho when Roxy, the former owner, decided she wanted more time with her husband and retired—my own husband, Seth, quickly swooping in and buying her out, incorporating it with his BDSM club, Club Alias. And even after the probing and exposing experience of pregnancy and the birth of my daughter, Luna, I still get a little embarrassed.

Maybe it's the fact that I was a virgin until I was twenty-four.

Or maybe it's because I kept myself sequestered and focused on my studies, then work before my sister and I made our escape from California and landed here on the East Coast several years ago. I hadn't been exposed to all the sexual stuff everyone else seems to find normal in TV shows, movies, and… well, everywhere you look, really. I was firmly planted in laboratories and cleanrooms while working as a chemical engineer, with no time for social media or even friends.

So how did I end up here, as the manager of a sex shop, you might ask?

I might not have had social media or friends, but I had my big sister. And as the only thing I cared about outside of my career, when Astrid needed my help to escape her abusive boyfriend, I was all in, a hundred percent. With her very life at stake, the way things were going, I knew we only had one chance to do it right. I quit my job, picked her up in the middle of the night, and after closing our eyes and letting fate guide our fingertip on the map, we drove straight to the other side of the country.

To a small military town called Ft. Vanter, where there was absolutely no use for a chemical engineer who focused on developing all-natural cleaning solutions.

And with that fancy degree and specialty, I was quickly labeled "overqualified" for literally every job I applied for around town… until Roxy took pity on me and hired me.

The virgin who had never even *seen* a vibrator in real life before.

But as fate would have it, during my very first week of working here, in walked Seth Owens, the—secret—owner of the local BDSM club, at which he was also the trainer in all things sex toys and equipment… although in a much more hands-on way than one would teach a new employee at a novelty store. But at that time, I didn't know that, and after a completely mortifying mishap, where my now sexy, goofy asshole of a husband pretended he was some regular guy stopping into a sex shop for the first time, Roxy spilled the beans and basically offered me up to the sex god as his newest disciple. She recruited him to teach me about all the things I was supposed to sell… and the rest, as they say, is history.

Along with my V-card.

I giggle at my last thought, my hand coming up to cover my lips, and receive a confused look from Christi much like my own a moment ago.

"Sorry. I squirreled there. Um. No. Not what I meant. The skin on these intimacy companions, it's supposed to feel incredibly real and unlike the silicone and other materials used for dildos and men's masturbators. I did a deep dive into this company's products, and judging by the compounds and componen—"

"Boss. As much as I love seeing you geek out about chemistry stuff, since you get so excited you don't even hesitate on words like 'dildos' or men's 'masturbators,' I've really got to get to class. I was just pickin'. I knew what you meant," she assures me with a smile, giving me a little wave before shoving open the tinted glass door.

I shake my head at her. "Have a good night, Chris."

She grins and makes her exit, but not before calling out her parting words for not only me but the customers walking inside to hear. "Text me after you squeeze her boobs!" And I stand there, red-faced, eyes wide, my mouth opening and closing like a guppy as the couple looks from her departing, laughing figure over to me.

"I—" My brain has shut down at the expression on their faces after registering it as worry, as if I plan to grope the well-endowed but fit black woman with long, thin braids decorated with gold beads. All I can do is shake my head in denial, hoping she understands Christi wasn't talking about her. But the words that finally leave my mouth don't help to convey that fact. "To see if they feel real."

She raises one perfectly sculpted eyebrow and turns her dark-brown eyes framed with extra-long, thick lashes up to her tall, handsome companion. The straight, white teeth of his big smile seem to light up not only his dark-tan face, but the entire store as he wiggles his eyebrows at her. She looks at me again and must see my natural reaction is the last of the human instincts to either fight, fly, or freeze, recognizing the misunderstanding.

She smiles then, hers even more powerful than the man's, because she has an endearing little gap just between her two front teeth, her lips painted a cool purple I couldn't dream of getting away with. "I mean, I didn't get them this big to look *real*, but if you want to squeeze them, go right ahead, honey."

My eyes widen even more, and my hands shoot up in front of me as if to ward her off. But then I realize it could look like I'm holding them up right at boob-squeezing level, and I jerk them back, my elbow hitting the display of individual, flavored condoms, sending them scattering to the floor like obscene little pieces of colorful confetti.

My eyes close behind my glasses then, so I don't see who walks through the door when the little bell dings at that moment.

But I sense him.

And knowing exactly who it is just by the way my body responds to his presence, my anxiety dipping and my heart rate calming, I'm both relieved and extra mortified for him to appear right in the middle of this embarrassing situation.

When I open my eyes, he's already knelt down next to me to pick the condoms up off the floor. As he looks up at me from his position on one knee, that ever-present mischievous twinkle in his hazel eyes, the smile that spreads across my husband's breath-stealing face makes me wonder how I could possibly think to describe anyone else's as beautiful, when it's this one all others are compared to.

"Breathe, doll," he murmurs, then stands to his full height, my head tilting back to keep eye contact with him.

"Christi short-circuited my brain again," I tattle, and he chuckles, leaning in for a soft, quick kiss.

"Well, luckily, she did it in front of friends instead of

strangers this time. Twyla, meet Antonio and Crystal. They're the owners of the place that opened up across the street from our building downtown. Antonio and Crystal Garcia, this is my wife, Twyla Owens," Seth introduces, his arm coming around my back to lead me toward the couple who came in before him. My first step stutters as he has to actually force my body to move in their direction, but I manage to reach my hand out in greeting on my own.

"Nice to meet you, Twyla." Antonio shakes my hand, but when I offer it to Crystal, instead of taking my hand, she dips forward a little, as if to set her huge breast in my palm, before jumping back and turning to press her front to Antonio's as they both burst into laughter at my loud squeak.

My hand is now pressed to my mouth as I look up at my husband, begging him with my eyes to save me.

"Okay, now I gotta know what I missed," he says instead, and I glare at him before dropping my arm.

"The intimacy companions came in today," I finally get out. "*That's* what Christi was telling me to squeeze." I look at Crystal again. "Not your… glorious décolletage." I attempt humor in order to get me out of this loop of embarrassment, or I'm afraid I'll be stuck in it for the rest of the day.

"Glorious décolletage," she repeats in a breathy, thick Southern accent before glancing up at her man. "I like the sound of that way better than 'your tig ole bitties.'" Which makes everyone laugh—including me, after the extra second it takes me to get it—and the tension leaves me. "But what the hell is an intimacy companion?"

"Um… it's like a… human-shaped, life-size… um… non-living partner for—"

"It's a sex doll," Seth inserts with a shrug. No shame. No

stutter. He just states it as if he's telling them the forecast after they asked what the weather's supposed to be like tomorrow. "Supposed to be super lifelike." He glances down at me. "You haven't felt them yet? I know you've been looking forward to them coming in."

My eyes widen once again and whip to the couple, and I rush to explain, "The skin. I've been excited to feel the texture of the skin. With my hand. Like… on the arm or something. Not any of the… intimate parts it comes with."

Crystal gives me a "you are the cutest little thing I've ever seen" smile before looking up at Antonio. "She's precious. Can I keep her?"

He chuckles and shakes his head. "You'll have to ask Seth if he wants you around her. You might corrupt her."

To that, my husband pulls me close, and when I look up at him, he lifts his hand to stroke his thumb along my jawline, sending a shiver down my neck and spine. "Believe me. If I wasn't able to, nobody can."

I melt against him as he pushes my glasses up my nose, then lets his finger trail down to the tip, as he's done since we first met. After a moment of just absorbing my perfect opposite, my person, who tells me he loves me unconditionally just the way I am, I straighten and look back at Crystal. "I always have room for another girlfriend, especially a local businesswoman. Even if all the women in my life have made it a competition between themselves to see who can embarrass me the most." I roll my eyes with a little laugh, totally used to being picked on. I know it's all in good fun. Plus, the same people who tease me are also my biggest protectors and supporters, and I know they wouldn't do it if they didn't love me.

But still, a teeny-tiny part of me wonders if Seth wishes I wasn't so… uncorrupted.

I know it's silly of me, since he tells me every single day how much he loves me. Even on the days I'm in full-on mom mode, hair in a messy bun, covered in God knows what after chasing around our preschooler for hours. He makes it a point to end each night with a shared shower, in which he soaps up and caresses my tired and kid-goo-smeared body, all while telling me how beautiful each part of me is. A tradition started after I grew self-conscious of my post-pregnancy and c-section-scarred form.

He'd have none of it.

The former sadist turned pleasure Dom inside Seth took over my hilarious and sweet life partner, and *Seven* put me to bed every night, sated and with no doubts about how he felt about my body. *"Different than it was before—but because of me, and still all mine,"* he always murmurs when his soapy hand skims over my scar before moving around my hip to possessively grip my ass cheek.

Yet, as much as he's made it perfectly clear he can't get enough of my physical form, doubt still creeps in when it comes to *me*. My personality. My shyness that never seems to fade, no matter how many years go by or the exposure to situations I feel other people would've grown used to and be unfazed by.

Because above all else, I worry I'm not the sub my former-professional-Dominant husband always dreamed of. Not because I'm not submissive, because God knows I am. Especially to this man, who is *so* deserving of his role. But because—like earlier with Crystal and Antonio—I freeze.

Often.

Even when told exactly how to do something, even in the

safe space Seven creates for us to play in, I frequently freeze, unable to follow his order, his gentle instruction, his clearly expressed desire. It's as if someone suddenly flips a switch inside me and turns my power off, and I'm stuck in whatever position I was in when that order was given, unable to move, to speak, to convey in any way what I'm feeling.

It's never fear. Especially not with Seth, but never with "Seven" either. Not once has my Dom punished me in any way for insubordination. Instead, he's always ended the scene and bundled me up with extra aftercare, so I'd know I hadn't disappointed him.

Maybe that's the problem, something whispers inside my mind, puzzling me, so I shoo it away.

No amount of reassurance from my husband, nor aftercare from my Master could possibly get rid of *every* doubt. And the one left inside my mind is powerful enough to make me wonder…

Is he truly happy, or just content?

"Sound good, doll?" Seth asks, squeezing me tightly to him to gain my attention.

I look up at him, feeling a little sullen and dazed from the path my thoughts had taken. "Hm? Sorry, I think I need some coffee," I say with a forced laugh as I stand up straight, taking my weight from Seth, and his brows furrow just slightly but enough I catch the worry there. "Managing this store on top of being a mom has made me single-handedly responsible for keeping the coffee shop next door in business, I swear."

Crystal chirps, "Girl, you ain't lyin'. We have two boys. And the business we're opening in the space downtown is a workout studio. Pilates, barre, pole dancing classes—you name it, I teach it. If it weren't for coffee and protein shakes, I wouldn't survive."

I feel my eyebrows shoot up my forehead. "Pole dancing classes?"

She smirks and nods. "Hell yes. You probably have no idea how strong a lady has to be in order to make it as an exotic dancer. We may make it look easy, but I promise—you know what a pecan looks like getting popped open by a nutcracker?" At my nod, she finishes, "These legs could do that to any meat-head at the gym's... well... meathead." She giggles sweetly, even though there's an evil little gleam in her eye. One glance at Antonio shows he feels nothing but pride in his woman's strength.

Crystal continues, "Which takes a lot of working out and muscle building. And since I stopped performing professionally when I got pregnant with our first son but didn't want to lose this body I worked so hard for, I decided to make an income by teaching new girls how to pole dance, which was a workout for myself as well. That was when we lived in Vegas. When we moved here, some ladies answered my ad about the classes who *weren't* dancers but wanted to learn anyway, whether for them-selves or to show off for their partner. And when they all loved it and said they'd be dropping their gym memberships to do my classes as their workout instead, I did some research and found out other small studios were offering pole dancing as an alterna-tive form of exercise. I kinda just went off what they were doing, and now, a few years later, I have enough members that I need the bigger space. Luckily, it's just right across the street from my original spot we got when we first moved to town."

"Across the street? That means—"

Seth interrupts, his ADHD hyping him up, "She was in the place on the other side of our security office."

"The one with the black-out curtains that are never open?" I ask, having wondered what that storefront was but had never taken the time to figure it out. My attention was always pulled to the *other* next-door neighbor of the Imperium Security office. Club Alias. Which also has an ominous-looking entrance.

"Yep. We didn't think our non-stripper ladies would want to be stared at from the sidewalk while they're trying to learn how to dance on a pole," Crystal explains.

Antonio adds, "Or cause traffic accidents on the one-way street we're on." He chuckles. "One peek through the window and there would be a daily pile-up. Especially if my woman was the one on the pole, giving instructions." He wiggles his eyebrows at her again, and she slaps his chest, rolling her eyes, even though I can see the pleased look in them at his compliment.

Another thought occurs to me then. "So that means your old space opened up. Do you know if it's still available? My sister has been toying with the idea of opening a ballet studio for a while now."

"As far as I know, it is. And even better, it wouldn't be much work to change it from an exotic dance studio to a ballet one. Since we're taking the poles with us and all." Crystal smirks, and we all laugh.

With that idea in my head to ponder on and present to Astrid, my earlier sullenness disappears, at least for now. We close up shop and put out the lunch-break sign, the four of us strolling next door for some much-needed coffee and more fun conversation to get to know each other.

All the while, a part of me still can't wait to get back to my store to feel up the sex doll.

CHAPTER 2

Twyla

"GUESS who went poopoo on the pottyyy!" Astrid sings in greeting as she opens her front door to let me in, and I glance from her bright, excited grin down to the dark-haired four-year-old with black-rimmed glasses that match my own. Her hazel eyes twinkle as she smiles at me, minus her father's mischief, since she's a little angel child who is never anything but sweet to her mommy.

I kneel right on the threshold and open my arms, and Luna runs into them, squeezing my neck tightly as I stand and pick her up. "You went all by yourself?" I ask her, my tone telling her how proud I am. She's had constipation issues since she was a baby, so going number two has been quite the obstacle, even though she's been potty trained since she was two.

She nods vigorously, her little baby-toothed smile making my heart clench. "Yes, Mama! And Uncle Neil got me popsicles after he saw the size of it. He said, 'Good grief, Luna. That's the size of a whole popsicle,'" she mimics in a deep voice. "And it made me want a popsicle, so he went and got me a whole box of them!"

I look over at my sister, trying to hide my slightly disgusted face from my daughter. Astrid reads the question in my eyes.

"Apparently, your husband likes to see what comes out of her so he can congratulate her on a job well done. Neil happened to walk by the bathroom just as she finished, so the next thing I knew, he was on FaceTime with Seth, showing him what was in the toilet."

I groan as I put Luna back on her feet, finally stepping into the house and shutting the door behind me. I reach down and pet Scout, Neil and Astrid's Australian Shepherd, who has come to greet me, as I tell my sister, "Oh, God. It's spreading. It was cute at first, when it was just Seth. But then suddenly she started demanding I take pictures of it to send him when he's at work if he doesn't answer a FaceTime call. And now she's getting you guys to do it too?"

Astrid gives me an evil grin. "You know kinks are hereditary, right? Our girl likes her praise… just like her mom and auntie!"

I smack her on the arm and shudder. "Stop it. She's four."

She holds her hands up. "Hey, don't blame me. We can't help we still love to be called a good girl. We just didn't realize how… *motivating* it was when we were young too."

"Gross." I give her a face as mine flushes, then hang my purse on the coat tree in the foyer and follow her into the kitchen, seeing Luna head in the direction of the living room with Scout, where I hear an episode of *Gabby's Dollhouse* playing from the TV. As I hike up one leg to sit on a barstool at the kitchen island, I sigh, slumping my upper half over the white marble.

"What's the matter, little sis? You've seemed down the past

couple of days. Everything all right?" Astrid asks, and I pull myself up to prop my head in my hand.

"I don't know. It's like… just a second ago. You so easily mentioned having a praise kink, as if that's a normal thing to slip into a conversation. And yes, I'm your sister, and we talk about *everything*, so like… why do I still get all red and embarrassed about it? Shouldn't I be immune to it by now?"

She waves her hand at me as she uses the other to open the refrigerator, as if to swat away my worries. "Oh, Twy. That's nothing to be concerned about. It's adorable that you still get all blushy over stuff like that. Your innocence is part of your charm." When I don't respond, she looks at me as she sets a variety of fresh fruits on the island between us, and her smile falls when she sees I have tears in my eyes. "Sis! What—? This is really concerning you?"

I swipe at the tears that spill when I shake my head, even though my mouth says, "I know it's silly."

Astrid hurries around the island and wraps her arms around my neck, pulling me down to squeeze my head to her chest. And like always, she's the one to take my glasses off my face so she can tighten her grip, surrounding me in her familiar, comforting scent. I have no choice but to allow her T-shirt to absorb my tears and whatever might be coming out of my nose.

She's the emotional one out of the two of us, and it's a rare occasion that I actually cry. But ever since we were young, this was the position she always put me in, as if she wanted to smother my sadness away.

"It's not silly, Twyla. None of your feelings are silly. Every single one of your emotions deserves validation, because you can't help the way something makes you feel. It's like a reflex.

You don't *make* yourself be sad. It just happens," she states, and I can't help but let out a little laugh.

"Is this what happens when you marry a therapist? You start sounding like one?" I ask her.

She squeezes me even tighter for a second before sitting me back up, her warm hands gripping my biceps for a moment to make sure I didn't get dizzy and fall off the stool from the change in altitude. She hands me my glasses, and when I get them in place, she swipes my dark hair out of my face and smiles gently at me. "Maybe. But this reaction makes me think you might need the real deal. You want me to see if Neil is finished with his last telehealth appointment of the day?"

My eyes go wide. "No! Astrid, no. I don't want to bother him. I don't want to keep you guys from what you have planned for this evening. I was supposed to just swing by and grab Luna as always, then—"

"We have zero plans for this evening. You are in no way a bother. And *something* made you come inside instead of hurrying home to start cooking dinner," she shuts me down.

I give her a monotone, "Seth is working tonight, so I was just going to grab Luna and me some Cane's. I really just wanted to see if you could help me figure out what to get him for his birthday."

My sister's face scrunches like it always does at the mention of fast food. "Do you know what those chickens' lives were like before they were sacrificed and boiled in vats of artery-clogging oils and fats, all for you to dip them in little cups of sugar and preservatives to feed my sweet, innocent little angel of a niece?"

"But it's okay for me?" I narrow my eyes.

"You don't care about you. But you care about Luna. So if I guilt you about *her,* maybe you'll actually listen and not fill either of your bodies with crap. You are what you eat, sis. You are what you eat," she repeats, slicing into a cantaloupe on the counter.

"Hey! I care about me. Have you forgotten I was once on a team coming up with a new all-natural formula for all-purpose cleaner?"

She scoffs. "Yeah, while fueling that brilliant brain of yours with Mickey D's and Weinerschnitzel."

This coming from the girl I used to eat super-cheap heat-up pizzas with every night when we were in hiding and our savings was dwindling. But once she moved in with Doc a year before they actually got together and insisted on cooking all his meals when he wouldn't let her pay rent, he'd get her whatever healthy and nutritious ingredients she needed from the grocery store. So long, Totinos.

I cross my arms and huff at her. "Then the Mickey D's and Weinerschnitzel must not be too bad for me, since I was so 'brilliant.'"

"Did someone say Weinerschnitzel?" comes Doc's deep voice, and I look over to see his giant form enter the kitchen. "Man, that place had the *best* chili dogs. I haven't had one of those since we went to Vegas to check out a BDSM club, when we were doing research for our own before it opened."

Astrid beams at her husband. "So like… fifty years ago, my love?"

He swats her on the ass, even though he has to be used to her poking fun of their age difference by now. "Goddess, I'm only forty-six."

She goes up on her tiptoes and puckers her lips, and he immediately obliges, but not because she still has the huge knife in her hand. He worships the ground my sister walks on, and I love that for her, especially since her ex never let her leave it, constantly beating her to the ground instead.

She lowers herself back on her bare feet and looks up at her man who's easily a foot taller than her. "Will you cut up the pineapple for me, Viking?" she says in a soft but sultry voice that has my face heating once again, and I look away from them.

I know this is just the way they are together, always. They live in their D/s dynamic twenty-four seven, and it works beautifully for them. I've never seen Astrid so profoundly happy, and it's all because of this man with the patience of a saint and the healing powers of some supernatural being from a fantasy book. And they were made for each other. He is, for lack of a better term, the Daddy Dom she's always needed, who takes the reins and guides her to accomplish everything she's always dreamed of. And she's the bright light in every room, a gift to anyone fortunate enough to be in her presence, the reward Doc earned by being a real-life superhero to so many people. He's her rock, calm but fiercely protective, and she brings life into his days when there wasn't any before. He makes any space safe for her to shine. As long as he's around, no one can dull her sparkle.

They'd be downright stupid to even try.

And that's exactly what that part of me is worried about, seeing this perfectly matched couple before me.

I don't think I'm that for Seth.

I don't think we're the type of opposites that complement each other, the way Doc and Astrid do.

Where Doc is Astrid's rock and makes her feel safe to be herself, and then Astrid's brightness has pulled Doc out of his shell—I feel like my shyness brings Seth down, and if the way I'm still so easily embarrassed is anything to go by, his extrovertedness hasn't rubbed off on me.

When I realize the room has gone quiet, I look up at my sister and brother-in law and see they're both staring at me with expressions of concern on their faces. Doc gives Astrid a nod, making me think she said something to him when I was spaced out, places a kiss on her forehead, and then rounds the island, holding his elbow out to me.

"Let's step into my office, shall we?" he prompts, and my chin wobbles before I place my hand in the crook of his arm, and he helps me off the stool.

CHAPTER 3

Twyla

"I'LL MAKE Luna some dinner. You go let Neil fix what's bothering you, and I'll get peace of mind knowing that my sweet niece will make it one more night without you poisoning her," Astrid tells me, and Doc turns his head toward her.

"Goddess," he rumbles, his warning tone saying more than words ever could.

She shrugs but looks a little chastised. "What? All the antibiotics they feed…." She doesn't finish her sentence, so he must've given her a look that stopped her in her tracks. "I'm sorry. You're right. Not the time. Love you, sis."

"Love you too," I murmur from the other side of her husband's big body, and he leads me toward his study.

He guides me to the overstuffed leather chair and gestures for me to sit, then he takes the matching couch in front of me, seeing my brow is furrowed when he looks over at me. "Are you comfortable?"

I nod. "Yeah. Of course. It's just… strange. At your office, *you* always take the chair, and we sit on the couch."

He gives me a small smile before saying gently, "This couch is… special. I don't allow anyone but your sister to sit on it now." And at the twinkle in his eyes, I can imagine what would make a couch special and reserved solely for one's wife, and my entire being flushes.

My hands go to my cheeks, and I press my cold fingers to my heated face. "This is what I'm talking about!" I cry out, my eyes filling with tears of frustration this time rather than self-pity.

"I missed what you and Astrid were talking about before the fast-food banter. Why don't you fill me in on what's bothering you?"

Instead of trying to calm myself and speak rationally, I blurt the first thing that pops into my head, which means it's the God's honest truth. "I don't think I'm good enough for my husband."

As stoic as Dr. Neil Walker normally is, I'm able to catch the split second his expression falters—his thick eyebrows dipping, his eyes narrowing slightly as there's a blip of confusion within them, the tiny backward jerk of his head as he's caught by surprise.

My husband is Doc's very best friend. His brother, though not by blood, and not just because the two of them are married to sisters. They're extremely close, the family they chose for themselves. He knows everything about Seth, down to his deepest, darkest secrets. Even more than I do, because of their many years of friendship and working together. Since that day Doc contacted Seth when he earned his master's from MIT at the age of twenty, after having graduated from high school when he was thirteen, offering the certified genius a position as the tech guru behind a team of mercenaries Doc was putting together. When Seth heard Doc's story, about why the world-renowned psychologist wanted to form a group of badass but stealthy mercs who focused their sights on rapists, he didn't even hesitate. He was all in. And ever since that very moment, they've been thick as thieves, literal partners in crime.

But no one knows that. To everyone else, they own just a normal, everyday security company—not at all involved with the untimely deaths that look like complete accidents.

So I guess I should take it as a good sign that Doc looks taken aback by my outburst, seeing as he knows Seth better than anyone. He would be the one my husband would go to if he needed to vent to someone about being unhappy or unsatisfied. But still.

"What brought about these feelings? Did something happen? Did Seth say anything that would lead you to believe he's disappointed with you in some way?" Doc asks, and his questions come rapid-fire, his voice tighter than I've ever heard it in the many *official* therapy sessions we've had at his office. His tone sounds almost… protective over me. Like he's about to call up Seth and give him a stern talking to, which is both heartwarming—knowing my brother-in-law cares about me, and enough that he'd defend me against his own best friend—and startling, because…

"No! Seth has never spoken an unkind word to me since the moment we met. And nothing happened. It's more… something *hasn't* happened," I tell him, seeing Doc immediately relax back in his special couch.

"All right. Good. Okay. Explain what you mean by something hasn't happened."

I push my glasses back up my nose and look upward, trying

to find the words to help me make him understand. "Well, it's like… take you and my sister for example. The two of you are so different from each other, but your differences seem to *fit* each other, like puzzle pieces. Where she has weakness, you seem to be extra-strong in that area. Where you're super chill and this… calming presence, Astrid—thanks to you—is back to being her bright, exuberant self. Yet you adore her wildness instead of being uncomfortable around it, and your chill doesn't, um… 'kill her vibe,' as Seth would probably say. Instead, it's like she gets you to live a little, and you make her feel as if she's not 'too much,' like she shouldn't dull herself down just because some people might find her extra-ness intimidating."

He nods. "And you feel that you and Seth aren't like this?"

"Right," I confirm.

He looks at me seriously. "Firstly, you do understand that every successful relationship is different, right? It's not always an opposites-attract type of—"

"Of course," I interrupt. "I see all sorts of couples come into the shop. But I'm not talking about the opposites-attract thing. I'm more concerned about the part where Seth and I haven't really… rubbed off on each other. Like how you calm Astrid when she may get overstimulated. Or how you get her to tone down a little when she could get herself in trouble or not realize when she's being overbearing. Like in the kitchen a minute ago. You didn't even *say* anything. You did some crazy Jedi mind trick, and she chilled on the bossy older sister thing she likes to do."

"Jedi mind trick?" He raises a brow. "Twy, you just disproved yourself by saying that." He grins. "Seth and his pop culture references have rubbed off on you enough that you now use them in conversation too." He chuckles at my look of surprise.

"Well... I.... No. Not the same, Doc. Totally not so simple a thing as that. I'm talking about bigger, more important influence. Like... um... you know, sexually," I finally get out, my face in flames once again. "See?" I screech, pointing to my blushing cheeks. "I can't even say the word 'sexually' without getting embarrassed! I manage a freaking adult novelty shop, and I'm married to a Dominant who owns a whole freaking BDSM club. I am completely submersed in sex stuff twenty-four seven, and yet I never get acclimated to it. Not even slightly. Shouldn't I be able to at least hold an adult conversation about... those things by now?"

"Twyla, you—"

I huff, cutting him off. "And yes, I've been this way since Seth met me, but I can't help but think he likely hoped I'd loosen up with time. Become more... adventurous, or at least be able to follow his orders without clamming up like I'm still the freaking virgin he first met. And I feel as if being this way is a downer." My eyes tear up again, my frustration quickly turning into a feeling of unworthiness. "He's so... perfect to me. Everything I never even knew to dream of. I could not be happier than I am with him as my husband. He's my everything, and the best dad in the whole world too. And I just...." I shake my head. "He is an incredible Dom. There hasn't been a single moment between us that made me think—not even for a second—that he shouldn't somehow be officially acknowledged as the world's greatest Dominant. If there was a competition, he would win it. Just like everything else, he's a genius in BDSM as well." My lip wobbles as I take a breath, and the last part comes out defeated. "And I'm not even close to being the sub he deserves."

The room is quiet for long seconds, and Doc gives me time to come to grips with finally speaking the things that have been bothering me for months, if not longer. It's always been in the back of my mind, but I was able to brush it off by telling myself it would just take time. It might take a while, but I'd get used to it. I'd be able to speak nonchalantly about this highly sexual world of ours, just like my husband and all our friends. Just like my sister.

But I'm still just as sensitive to it as I was the day I started working at Toys for Twats.

A box of tissues appears in my line of vision that had been aimed at my lap. I take one, thank Doc quietly, and use it to wipe beneath my glasses.

"Twy, with this, I feel it'd be beneficial to you if I spoke more as your friend than as your therapist. Even though it would be inappropriate for any Dominant other than your own to speak to you about such things, in this case, I'm coming to you more as your husband's best friend, who is also your friend, letting you in on some things you might not realize. Do I have your consent for this conversation to be worded in a casual, familiar way instead of as a professional psychologist with his patient?" Doc asks, and my heart swells even more toward my brother-in-law. He's such a wonderful man, and I'm so happy my sister gets to spend the rest of her life with this incredible human.

I nod. "Yes. Please. I'd really like that."

He gives me a half-smile before he begins. "I knew Seth for many years before you two Quill girls came into our world. And while he's always been the funny, goofy, good-natured person we all know and love, there was also this… damaged part of him before he met you. He's always been a highly skilled Dominant who's a stickler for the rules of this lifestyle, never breaking the trust of those who submitted to him. But inside, *Sadist* was the Dominant role he most identified as. And he had to be selective with the subs he played with, in order to be sure they were highly masochistic and *wanted* his level of sadism. But you healed that part of him, so he no longer feels the needs of a sadist, at least not nearly as strongly."

I shift in my seat, not really hearing the last sentence he said, unable to control the jealousy I feel when I allow myself to think about my husband's former submissives. When we first got together, the sole thing I cared about was making sure I would be his one and only. He's the head trainer at the club, after all, where his style of teaching was always very hands-on before he met me.

My main concern was that he'd want to continue with that same teaching approach, even while being in a relationship with me. I feared he would say yes to subs who propositioned him to play for the first time, to experience submitting to a literal Master, or that he'd agree if former students and partners wanted to have another go. He'd always been a single man with no long-term sexual partners, so I didn't know if he wanted or even had the ability to be in a monogamous relationship.

I made it clear that I didn't have it in me to share him, so if he wanted to be with me, I needed him to be faithful. I needed to be the only woman in his life, the only one he'd ever touch, kiss… love.

I thought it would be a big ask.

To my surprise, it's exactly what he wanted, and he craved the same thing from me. Although I thought it was silly he even *thought* I might someday allow, or even want, another man to touch me. I was a twenty-four-year-old virgin who finally found the one man I wanted to give myself to. Him. No one else would ever come close.

"Are you all right?" Doc asks, pulling my eyes up to meet his laser-blue ones watching me closely.

I blush again, but this time from shame. "I know it's immature, but I get jealous when I think about his previous partners. Ignore me." I wave off my emotions, but he surprises me by asking another question instead of continuing his story.

"Your feelings should never be ignored, Twy. Every emotion you feel is valid. So will you explain what you experience where Seven's past subs are concerned?"

I smile inside, remembering Astrid saying something very similar when I got here earlier. Another example of how Doc is always rubbing off on her in a positive way.

"My jealousy, possessiveness, whatever you want to call it, ever since we established our monogamous relationship undoubtedly comes from my self-doubt in being a good submissive. I can't help begrudging his former subs, because nothing could ever make me believe any of them were as terrible at it as I am. They were all incredibly sexy and confident, I'm sure, knowing exactly how to please this… professional Dom, the owner of the exclusive establishment they were deemed worthy enough to be members of. They were vetted, hand-picked, given a very hard-earned seal of approval. But I, on the other hand, was basically just… grandfathered in. He wanted me in, so even if I'm unworthy of being there, I still get in the door." I cringe.

I've never been one to feel so self-deprecating. I've always been a confident person, because I always excelled at what was important to me. My studies, my career as a chemical engineer, and being a good, loving little sister. But all of that disappeared the moment we crossed the California state line. Well, except the loving little sister part. Gone were my studies. Gone was my chosen career path I had been so passionate about. And instead, I did what was necessary to survive and keep Astrid safe. Which I have zero regrets about. I just… lost myself in the process.

"Okay, again, coming to you as your husband's best friend, I need to let you in on something. Once I do that, then we can address what's personally going on with you and hopefully be able to start working on fixing it," Doc tells me, and I nod, then lean forward in the chair, both anxious and excited to hear what he has to say.

"First of all, Seth is obsessed with you. You see that, don't you?"

I smile. "He does act quite enamored. Which I don't understand—"

He interrupts, "It's not an act, Twy. And you don't have to necessarily understand why. You just need to believe it. He's not only in love with his wife. He is infatuated by you, everything that makes you *Twyla*. You said it yourself—you've seen the types of women at Club Alias. You've met some of his former students. And he was once a highly sought-after Dominant. I'm sorry to cause you any type of discomfort, but to put it bluntly, yes, he could've chosen any one of those women to not only be his sub, but to be in *any* kind of long-term relationship with."

I swallow thickly and sink back in the chair, trying in earnest to keep my tummy from bubbling with the acid I feel starting to churn.

"But he never did. Not even once," Doc continues. "Not a single time did Seth mention a woman by name in all the years I've known him. Not one time did he say anything about a sub causing him to feel any sort of emotion. But the very day he met *you,* he told all of us—Corbin, Brian, *and* me—that he met a girl named Twyla, and she made him feel 'weird.'"

I can't help it. I let out a laugh as my heart expands even more for the man I married. Knowing him the way I do, "weird" would've been a big deal for him to feel, *and* for him to confess to his closest friends. It would've been startling for those guys to hear it coming from him as well. As goofy as the man is, and as much as he loves to quote movies and such, Seth is off-the-charts intelligent, with a vocabulary that is astounding. For him to be unable to describe what he was feeling as anything but "weird," meant it was an emotion he'd truly never experienced before.

And he felt it for *me.*

"I can see you get what a big deal that was for everyone there that day, so I'm going to take it one step further. I talked to him throughout the entire beginning of your relationship. Each step of the way, he came to me to help him decipher what he was thinking, wanting. Courting a woman was something he'd never done before. Every single action and feeling he was experiencing was brand-new territory. And he was determined to get it right. He knew from the start that you were special, and he wanted to make damn sure he didn't do anything that would fuck up his chance to be with you. Once Seth decided you were meant to be his, that's it. You were all that mattered. Anyone and anything else that could possibly keep that from becoming his reality, he shoved it all away. And it was for *good,* Twyla." He looks at me seriously. "You *have* to know that about your husband. Once he makes a decision, it's final. There are no takebacks."

I nod. "Oh, I know that for sure. But there's nothing to say that he can't regret a decision he's made. There's no rule that states he can't get bored with me, just because he may stick to his guns and not seek anyone else. I know for a fact Seth—and Seven for that matter—would never cheat on me. It's against his moral code. No matter what, he wouldn't allow himself to break that vow. But that doesn't mean he can't be unhappy with me. It doesn't mean he can't be disappointed that this woman he'll be faithful to for the rest of his life isn't good enough for him in bed. That I'm not learning to be a better submissive. That I'm not catching on to the things he's tried to teach me. That I freeze when he gives me an order and am physically unable to carry out what he's asked of me."

As my bottom lids lose their battle against my tears once more, I see my brother-in-law sink a little to the side so he can prop his elbow on the arm of the couch and rub his beard-covered chin between his thumb and pointer finger. His eyes are narrowed, and I can tell he's not really looking at me but internally. Trying to solve the puzzle I've laid out in front of him.

He murmurs to himself, "Secure in relationship, but not...."

After a moment, he nods and sits up, his bright blue eyes clear as he speaks to me this time. "This is purely a matter of self-doubt, insecurity in yourself and your abilities, and also... this stress reaction of freezing." Those eyes of his gleam with... excitement? "I can help you, Twy. If you can agree to face it head-on and just trust me—even if what I tell you to do sounds silly, or embarrassing, or completely pointless—then I promise we can fix these negative feelings and responses of yours."

I started nodding vigorously the moment he said "I can help you." If my brilliant therapist says he knows how to fix my broken self-esteem and stop me from freezing with the man I love, then I will do my part, whatever it takes.

"I'm embarrassed *all* the time, Doc. Can't get any worse, right?"

CHAPTER 4

Twyla

WRONG. Very… *very* wrong.

My eyes are narrowed behind my thick-framed glasses, my face stuck in a mask of fascination and fear as I watch my new friend Crystal freefall from the ceiling in a graceful upside-down pose, then catch herself on the silver pole a mere inch before her head hits the floor.

But the fear in my expression has nothing to do with the extremely talented and professional pole-dance instructor's safety. She's clearly got this.

No. It's because, apparently, I'm here in her new studio to get on one of those spinning, floor-to-ceiling, cylindrical death traps myself.

Astrid lets out a whoop and applauds, and all the sound my mind blocked out when I first realized what Doc, my sister, and Crystal expect of me today comes rushing back in, making my heart race faster than it already had been.

Come to find out, Seth had taken Crystal and her husband

around to meet several people after we left the coffee shop and I went back to work yesterday. Which I didn't know about until this morning.

After my session with Doc and before Luna and I went home, he had a quick, private discussion with Astrid in the kitchen—who I saw jump up and down excitedly before covering her mouth—while I helped my daughter gather her things in the living room. My feeling of foreboding was damn near tangible, especially when the beautiful couple approached me cautiously, like I'd choose that moment to learn how to run instead of freeze when stressed.

Astrid stood next to Doc, clearly trying to stop a grin from lifting the corners of her full, pink lips, as he told me, "Okay, Twy. It's all set. Tomorrow morning will be your first assignment. Your sister will accompany you for moral support and accountability."

My apprehensive stare shifted between the two of them.

"So then why does she have that evil little glint in her eye?" I asked him.

He glanced down at his wife, and she tilted her head back to peer up at him, her face a mask of pure innocence as she shrugged, then she looked down at me once again, the wickedness reappearing right back where it had been.

He swatted her on the butt, and she yelped then giggled.

"You don't worry about her. Just go with her when she arrives to pick you up in the morning. And remember… trust me." He didn't break his impenetrable stare until he finally received my nod of agreement.

"So *this* is what I get for trusting your husband?" I murmur to Astrid as Crystal cuts off the thumping music and walks over to us.

I'm in black biker shorts that hit me mid-thigh, and a black sports bra topped with a loose T-shirt that reads, **Chemistry. It's like cooking, but don't lick the spoon**, after Astrid arrived this morning, took one look at my jeans, and told me I'd need to change into something I could work out in. I traded my bottoms and kept on the shirt, slipping my feet into tennis shoes rather than the flip-flops I had on, thinking we were going to Doc and Astrid's beloved gym. Maybe he wanted me to take a yoga class or something to… calm my chi? Wasn't that a thing? Weren't yoga classes supposed to be good for centering yourself and letting go of negative feelings? I could buy that. No problem. I'd just choose a mat hidden in the back where no one could see how unathletic I am.

Seth and I moved into a house close to the other couple right before I gave birth to Luna, since our loft wasn't big enough for the three of us, and we didn't want to raise our baby right above a sex club. I loved living just up the street from my big sister. But as she stopped at the stop sign, instead of making a right out of our neighborhood to head toward the gym as I expected, Astrid turned left. I glanced in the back seat at Luna in her car seat, before facing the blonde menace beside me as I nervously asked, "Where are we going?"

"You'll see" was all she said in a singsong voice.

When we parked on the street right across from Imperium Security and Club Alias, I was completely confused. And then a feeling of dread took over when Astrid hopped out of the car, opened the back door, unhooked Luna, and slammed it closed with her hip before skipping with her niece over to the sidewalk next to my door. Where I saw her point to the still-signless storefront closest to us.

And that's when it hit me where we were going.

"Astrid Walker!" I hissed as I stepped out and closed the door, hearing the car lock. "We cannot take a baby into a strip club!" My panic made the wrong words come out, and my sister jumped on the opportunity to correct me.

"One, she's not a baby. She's four. And two, it's not a strip club. It's a workout studio. Plus, she's not staying. She has a playdate with Corbin and Vi's little ones up the street at the children's discovery place so you can focus. See? There she is now." Astrid looked over my shoulder and waved, and I turned to spot Vi walking quickly toward us on the sidewalk.

When she was near, she reached out to Luna, who immediately squealed, jumped into her arms, and pressed her cheek to Vi's, squishing their faces she hugged her auntie so tightly. "I've got her, Mama. And *you've* got *this*. Imma hurry back though, because I don't want to leave the kids unsupervised. Love y'all," our best friend—and the wife of one of the other team members—assured, and then she disappeared through the door she had come from.

I looked at Astrid, my face showing my annoyance. "Does *everyone* know what I'm being subjected to?"

She shook her head. "Of course not. Just us girls and Doc. Because we have a plan."

"What plan?"

"Well, it's not fully formed yet, but part of it is to make sure you have something special to give your husband for his birthday."

And with that, she grabbed my arm and hauled me into Crystal's studio, who locked the frosted door behind us with a grin.

Now, as the woman stands in front of me—sans all the makeup, false eyelashes, and cleavage from yesterday and instead wearing one of those high-impact sports bras that zip up the front to her collarbones—that whole freeze thing I'm known for kicks into high gear. As sweet as Crystal is, I get the impression she has the ability to flip a switch and could suddenly become a badass drill sergeant, running this place like a boot camp if she chose to.

Much like my sweet, goofball husband, who at the drop of a hat can conjure the intimidating Dominant, Seven, who lives just beneath his always-sinfully-beautiful surface.

I wonder if Crystal has a name for that other persona I somehow sense within her.

What was your stripper name? I wonder, and when she asks, "What? Crystal isn't stripper enough as it is?" with a laugh, I want the wooden floor to open up and swallow me as I realize I asked that question out loud.

My face goes up in flames, and I rush to apologize. "Oh my God, Crystal. I'm so sorry. I did not mean to say that. I swear, I was just thinking about how you're so nice, but there's something about you that tells me you could probably be a tough trainer and hurt me if you wanted to. And then I thought about how my husband—" I cut my rambling off abruptly, because no one is supposed to know that Seth Owens is Seven, owner of an exclusive BDSM club. "Uhhh… he has like… this alter ego when he's uhh… goofing off that he's named. And I was like, I wonder if Crystal has a name for this badass I think she's hiding inside, and somehow that came out of my mouth as 'stripper name.'"

She exchanges a look with Astrid, and then the two of them fall into a fit of laughter, making me feel a little nauseous I'm so humiliated.

"Honey, I believe you mean my Domme name, which you actually met me briefly by at the New Year's party at the club.

My husband—my sub—introduced me to you as Countess. I have this… blood thing." She shrugs with a gleam in her dark eyes, and then her voice lowers and slightly deepens, taking on a sensual tone that makes me hold my breath. "You must be a very good submissive to so easily pick up on my role, which I've spent years perfecting the ability to hide… unless I don't want to."

I swallow thickly, but shockingly, I don't blush or freeze. In fact, something about her tone is soothing, makes me feel safer in this space than I had just moments ago. And for her to compliment my instincts, going so far as to say I must be a very good submissive, heals a little piece of my broken self-confidence in that role.

Maybe I have picked up and learned more than I realize?

When I've discovered a lot of my anxiety has disappeared, I meet her knowing eyes and smile gratefully. "Thank you for saying that. And it's nice to know someone from the club on the outside. That's definitely a relief," I tell her. "I can't believe I didn't recognize you. I always thought the little masks and stuff we wear there would be ineffectual if we met another member at like… the grocery store or something. No way it could be like Clark Kent and his fake glasses. Surely all those people weren't fooled. The hero they always saw blasted all over the news and stuff, and they couldn't tell it was him just because of a pair of glasses? Come on. But I guess…."

Crystal holds up a finger and sashays over to the table holding the Bluetooth speaker her phone is connected to. She taps and scrolls along the screen, then comes back over to show me a photo. I can tell by the decorations it was taken at the New Year's Party right across the street.

Now knowing it's her, I recognize Crystal's voluptuous figure and the shape of her full lips that are painted a matte black in the photo. She's not smiling in it, instead wearing a closed-lipped smirk that tells me my new friend might lean toward the sadistic end of the spectrum along with her "blood thing," so her telltale little gap isn't showing. The rest of her, from head to toe, is clad in a skin-tight, shiny latex bodysuit the likes of Michelle Pfeiffer's *Catwoman*, minus the ears. Definitely not like Halle Berry's—her costume was almost as identity-revealing as Superman's glasses. The only skin Crystal's bodysuit shows is from the slits for her mouth and eyes, much tinier than either of the villain's costumes had.

I tilt my head, look up at her and her thick braids, then back down at the photo. My face must show I'm trying to solve a puzzle, because she chuckles and asks, "What?"

I look back up from her phone, my voice full of wonder. "Halle Berry has a pixie cut. How do you fit *all that hair* under there?"

After she bursts out laughing, slapping her thigh and closing out her screen, she answers without truly revealing anything, "Black girl magic."

Astrid shakes her head at me. "Plus, Halle had grown out her hair by the time she played Catwoman, sis. Remember? It was pretty long and curly during the parts she wasn't in the suit, when she was her counterpart, Selina Kyle. And Michelle Pfeiffer too. She had all those voluminous curls I envied." She lets out a dreamy sigh.

I nod, recalling that now but still not understanding the physics of Crystal getting all those heavy-looking braids to lie perfectly flat and secure under that tight mask.

"But bravo on not one but two DC references. I'll have to tell

Seth he needs to give his woman some kind of reward." My sister winks, and I roll my eyes.

"He was on a mission to prove to me why Marvel is superior to DC Comics, even though I never argued or had an opinion either way." I don't even have time to blink before something occurs to me. "Hey, wait. Did *you* know Crystal from the club?" I ask Astrid.

"Of course. Neil met them in Vegas years ago. Like… before the guys opened Club Alias," she says with a shrug, as if that explains everything.

But my mind just isn't connecting the dots. "So… huh?"

Crystal takes pity on me. "How about I tell you the Cliff's Notes version of my life story while we stretch, before we start our lesson?"

I nod, and she leads us over to the mat-covered floor that has six of the rotating poles seeming to sprout out of them. She tells us to each pick the pole that speaks to us, and naturally, I choose the one that's closest to the back wall and behind my sister.

"Not that one," comes Crystal's authoritative voice, and I gulp. "Over here, sweet girl, where I can see and help you. *This one* is the one speaking to you today." She points to the pole closest to her, at the front of the "class," and as the sub in me senses the Domme in her once again, somehow, I follow her directive without pause, actually finding relief, feeling safer, by being closer to her instead of hiding.

But being the clearly experienced and respectful Dominant she is—Club Alias wouldn't have allowed her to become a member otherwise—she doesn't offer me praise the way one would in an established D/s relationship.

Firstly, that would require consent; a conversation would need to take place where I'd give her, a Domme, permission to speak to me, a sub, with authority—to give me orders, to reward or punish me, et cetera. It would be my choice, if I wanted to submit to her in any way, whether she *identifies* as a Dominant or not. Consent is required for everything between Dominants and submissives, right down to her calling me pet names. That one, though, I've always chosen to pay less attention to, since a lot of the time it's a cultural thing to call people by terms of endearment, especially here in the South. A cultural thing I happen to adore.

Secondly, we are both in our own D/s relationships, so she'd actually have to ask *my Dom's* permission to address me in her Domme persona. A Dominant could either answer yes or no right off the bat—which Seven would and has before, if it was a male—or they could choose to have a private discussion with their submissive first, to see what the sub's opinion might be. But ultimately, it would be my Master's decision.

But even though no conversation has taken place between any of us about consent, there's just something about *Crystal*—not Countess—that makes me want to let her lead me. And it's in no way sexual. Not even slightly. There is a certain confidence—not cockiness—and trustworthiness I sense in her that tells me I'm safe in her hands, in whatever she wants to teach me. An instinctive thing, as she pointed out when we first arrived. She might have spent years trying to perfect her ability to hide her Dominance unless she willed it to come out and play, but there are just some things, things that are soul-deep, that a person has no control over. And apparently, my instincts as a submissive have been honed enough, trained enough, or are just soul-deep enough, that I can pick up on what Crystal naturally exudes.

And it's in this moment I realize something about this "assignment" Doc gave me.

"This isn't about me learning how to pole dance, is it?" I ask, my voice strong, my face remaining its un-flushed temperature and color, as I look at my instructor, then my sister, and then back to Crystal. All of us are seated on the cushioned floor, each straddling our own pole, legs out straight in front of us, using the silver metal between our calves to pull ourselves into a deeper fold to stretch.

Astrid and I had followed Crystal's instruction without her even saying a word.

The two women eye each other for a second, smile knowingly, and then turn to me.

When neither responds, I elaborate, "This is about me discovering I *have* learned things. I *have* picked up lessons along the way, without me being totally conscious of it. Isn't it?"

Astrid is the first to speak. "Neil and I thought it was interesting that you weren't cognizant of the little habits you've picked up from Seth, simple things, like referencing movie characters during conversations, when you *never* would've done that before you met him." She shrugs. "So, he wondered if it could possibly be the same situation going on with your lack of confidence as a submissive. Like, maybe you just don't *realize* how much you've actually learned, how much you know, about your role as a sub. I mean, it's not like you've been handed a test and been graded. A teacher hasn't returned your answers, showing the ones you got right and the ones you got wrong, confirming your knowledge or lack thereof. So how could you know if there are things you need to work on, or if you're an ace?" She grins, leans toward me, and boops my nose with her pointer finger. "My nerdy little sis."

I'm too stunned to swat her away.

I look at Crystal. "And you were in on this?" My voice

sounds a little accusatory, even though I'm feeling quite grateful to all parties involved.

She holds up her hands in defense, shaking her head slowly. "Hey, now. When Dr. Neil Walker asks you to help him out, I don't care *how* dominant you are. You do what he wants and feel honored he chose *you* to do it for him."

I nod, conceding easily. "That's fair."

She looks me dead in the eye then, and my tummy does a little flip. "But seriously, girl. I was genuinely taken aback when he called last night—not because he called, but because of what he was calling *about*. What he told me about the woman he was needing my help with did not match the sub I remembered meeting on New Year's Eve. She couldn't have been the one I saw with her husband in their store yesterday, or the one I hung out with at the coffee shop either."

My brow furrows, not understanding what she means, since those women were all one and the same—me.

She switches up her position on the mat, and we follow her lead almost unconsciously. She explains further without pause. "The *sub* I met at Club Alias—perfect classic positioning while mingling in a crowd of other Doms and subs. Slightly behind her Dom, head marginally bowed, relaxed features. I did notice your tight grip on his arm, but that could've always been by his order, his preference or what the two of you agreed upon in your dynamic. But when he introduced you that night, you met my eye politely and nodded but didn't offer your hand, which is common in our community. My first impression of you was that you were a highly trained and gloriously obedient submissive who looked perfectly natural and *happy* in your role."

I'm speechless, hearing her recollection of our initial introduction during the New Year's party. I *was* super happy that night. I didn't put much thought into the way I stood or acted, not at all, really. I always just feel the most comfortable right there, with my tall and strong husband leading the way, my hands around his bicep, reveling in his powerful strength I can always sense beneath the surface of his long-sleeved black Henley and light-tan skin. I try to absorb it into myself, since I've never been big on crowds. I'm definitely an introvert, while he is a hundred percent an exhibitionist.

We all switch the leg we're stretching, and Crystal continues. "The *wife* I observed with her husband at the store yesterday looked to him for guidance and comfort with nothing but love and trust in her eyes. Like she had no doubt he'd know exactly how to make her feel better in the stressful or embarrassing situation she found herself in. And he looked at her like she was the center of his entire universe. Girl, when he wasn't staring at you with hearts in his eyes like Cupid just shot him in the ass with an arrow, he was lookin' like that wolf in the cartoons, with his tongue rolled out across the table, you know? Anyway, he alternated between looking like he wanted to kiss your face or make you ride his. No in between."

My eyes widen, and my hand slaps over my mouth after I let out a very unladylike squawk. Her description had started out so sweet.

My sister, on the other hand, is on her back, knees pulled up to her chest, her hands covering her eyes, but she's dying of laughter.

Her laugh is infectious though, and every time she tries to stop, she fails, bursting out loudly once again, which sets off my giggles, and I hear Crystal start to cackle as well, probably at us finding what she said so hilarious.

When we finally get control of ourselves, Astrid having to

wipe off the tears that fell from the outer corners of her eyes to her hairline, Crystal inserts with faux haughtiness, "As I was sayin'," before getting us back on track in her stretching routine. "There was no way *that wife* could possibly think her husband thought of her as anything less than absolutely perfect."

My face warms for the first time since I accidentally asked her what her stripper name was when we first arrived here. But it's not from embarrassment or shame or anything of the sort. It's from the pleasurable heat that started in my chest and spread outward, from another woman telling me what she saw when my husband looked at me.

What, probably, all women see when my husband looks at me.

What all the submissives at Club Alias see…

When my Dom looks at me.

CHAPTER 5

Seth

"GUESS WHAT I LEARNED TODAY," my beautiful—*sweat-stained?*—wife prompts the moment she and our mini-her walk in the door.

"How to sweat outside our bedroom?" I ask her, the last word said against her lips just before I kiss her and take the bags she's carrying. She pokes me in my abs as she pulls back, shifting her eyes to Luna, then back to me with a "little ears are listening" look. But we don't have to worry about filtering for more than a second before Luna runs off to her room.

"Anyway," she singsongs. "Today, I learned that if you go to Vegas to become a showgirl, traditionally, you start in one of the exotic dance clubs. If you get hired at one of the clubs right on The Strip, it's apparently a big deal, since they only want the most beautiful dancers who can do all the super cool tricks on the pole. And if you last a while there, it's very impressive on a resume, just in case you audition for one of the big shows in the huge casinos. Also, a lot of the talent scouts will go to those clubs to spot any hidden gems they think would fit what they're looking for."

I listen to her enthusiastic tale as we both empty the groceries from the bags onto the counter, and then I grab the can opener out of the drawer to get started on dinner.

"Are you trying to say you're leaving me to go strip on The Strip, doll?" I smile, but when I glance up at Twyla, she looks utterly horrified. I forgot she doesn't know I'm actually in on what's going on with her and Doc's therapy—part of a contract she signed when she became an official member of Club Alias.

At first, I believe that look is in response to her leaving me. But what she says next shuts that down *and* pisses me off.

"As if I'd stand a chance. Who'd spend their hard-earned money to see this? Plus, I couldn't even hold myself up today. An exotic dancer, I was not meant to be." She shakes her head. "Plus, you're stuck with me, husband," she adds, making me feel better about that part at least.

She was opening the package of chicken breasts while she spoke, gesturing to herself from head to shorts, not paying attention to my immediate change in demeanor, so she's startled when she feels my hand wrap around her throat from behind as I pull her back to my front. Her little squeak makes my dick jump inside my basketball shorts, and I know she feels it against her plump ass, even through her modest biker shorts. They're long but they're thin, and my cock nestles right between her cheeks when I squat enough to speak quietly into her ear.

"You feel that, doll?" At her frantic nod when I grind into her, I tell her, *"Me."* My hand tightens a little around her throat as I lick along the salty shell of her ear. *"I* would spend every cent of my hard-earned money to see *this*." My free hand fills itself with her soft flesh, first over her sports bra, and then beneath it so I can feel the weight of her breast. My cock hardens even more.

She whimpers, so I loosen my grip on her neck slightly, hearing her suck in a breath before she moans quietly when my other hand trails from her tit to her hip. My fingers dig in there, and like my good little doll, she gives in to my subtle shifts in pressure leading her to bend over the kitchen island.

A flashback of our first time together fills my mind, and I smirk as I glimpse the package of chicken next to where I have my wife's face now pressed to the cold marble.

I bend over her back, pushing the air out of her lungs with my weight. "What have I told you about speaking badly about my wife's body?"

She nods. "I'm sorry. I just meant I'm weak. I promise, Master." Her breathy voice and the rush of words make me groan, and if I didn't hear the pitter-patter of little feet heading in our direction, I would've dropped Twyla's shorts to feel if she was as wet as my pre-cum has made me. Instead, I quickly shift my hand from her neck to her shoulder and help her stand up, wrapping both my arms around my woman tightly in a hug and kissing her cheek as she settles against my front once again.

We learned long ago that physical closeness after submitting is a necessity for my wife. Otherwise, she experiences debilitating sub-drop, which she can't control. The few times I had to rush to work right after an enthusiastic quicky, she wasn't able to get out of bed. At first, I joked that I wore her out so good she couldn't move after I left. But when she elaborated that it almost felt like a depressive episode, like she was suddenly overcome with sadness and loneliness and felt like she just didn't have the drive to get up—*not* referring to physical strength—I knew right away what she was experiencing.

Even though I was never one to have to worry about aftercare with my previous submissives, I understood and recognized sub-drop from my years of devouring every morsel of information pertaining to this lifestyle. It's why, before Twyla, I always discussed with the sub before playing that, if they wanted, another Dominant could come in right after a scene, so they could receive proper aftercare, just not from me.

But this is my wife. Mine. And with this little bit of aftercare—that I have no problem giving my amazing woman, since I'll use any excuse just to touch her—it assures her I'm not mad at her, that my aggression came from my lust for her, and that she did a good job allowing me to dominate her. She gets all of that, not a single word spoken, just from a tight and prolonged hug, which is easily done right in front of our little girl as she walks in asking about a snack.

"You can have some goldfish crackers, baby, but not a lot. Dinner will be ready fast," Twyla tells her, her voice a little shaky but clear. When Luna skips over to the pantry to grab one of the individual packs of Flavor Blasted Goldfish, I feel my wife give me all her weight, allowing herself to fully relax, knowing I've got her. Luna brings the red bag over to us, and Twyla opens the perforated packaging easily before handing it back to our girl. Then she hurries off to her room once again, completely clueless of what's really going on, merely thinking Daddy is just giving Mama love like he always does.

After a moment of soaking each other in, Twyla puts her weight back on her feet and taps my forearm, telling me she's all good. I loosen my hold enough so she can spin to face me, and I link my fingers behind her back, not ready to let her go quite yet.

"Did Doc tell you where I was going today?" she asks, reaching up to push her glasses up her nose.

"He said you were going with Astrid to try out Crystal's pole-dancing workout. I assume she's the one who gave you the education on the Las Vegas showgirl scene?" I prompt, being elusive about everything I know that pertains to her assignment today. The last thing I want to do is embarrass Twyla or make her feel anything negative about getting help for something she felt more comfortable seeking from a professional. While I wish she'd open up to me about what she's feeling, I know that will come in time, when she's ready. I'm just thankful I have the heads-up I do, so I can be conscious of not making matters worse and by subtly helping in any way I can, as her husband and as her Dom.

"Yes! That woman has led a fascinating life. First, she was a ballet dancer with training in gymnastics. And when she turned eighteen, she moved to Vegas with dreams of being a showgirl. More specifically, a dancer in a burlesque show. She grew up obsessed with *The Girls Next Door,* which I guess is an old show about three women who were Hugh Hefner's girlfriends, and—"

"Wait, you know who Hugh Hefner was?" I ask, impressed, since she really only knows pop culture icons from the things *I've* shown her.

She gives me a deadpan look. "I *am* from California. We lived only like… an hour from the Playboy Mansion. He was unavoidable."

I tilt my head and concede, "That's fair."

"Anyway, Crystal doesn't seem to have *ever* had any self-consciousness issues. She gives exhibitionist vibes for sure, and I admire that. Anyway, she learned the ins and outs, was immediately hired at one of the clubs right on the Vegas Strip, and after four years of making tons of money there, a talent scout approached her to be in a vampire-themed burlesque show that was a permanent fixture at The Stratosphere for *years*," she gushes, and I love that she's so impressed with her new friend.

"Now, the question is... did she jump at the opportunity because of her blood fetish, or did she take the job and gain the blood fetish from working for the show?" I wiggle my eyebrows at her.

She gasps and swats my arm before spinning around to get started on seasoning the chicken. "That's another thing I learned today, you butthole. I had no idea, when we were hanging out with them yesterday, that I had already met them at Club Alias! I felt so silly when she let me in on that little tidbit."

I drag my hand along her ass as I walk back over to the canned vegetables I was opening before getting distracted by my ever-present obsession with my wife. "Sorry, doll. I didn't want to make you feel awkward just throwing it out there that they were members and now knew who we were out in the wild. I wanted you to get to know her, since I had a feeling you'd really like her, without having to worry about what she might've seen us doing in whatever precarious position I've had you in on different occasions."

It was a *rare* occasion I did a public scene with my doll, and nothing over the top or that would expose too much of her body, but the scenes we *have* done on display were some of the hottest things I've ever experienced.

She smiles, looking at me with relief in her eyes. "It's times like this I don't understand why there are women who absolutely *refuse* to see the benefits of allowing a man to make decisions on their behalf."

"Oh yeah?" I ask, dumping the peas into a small pot and turning the stove on.

She nods. "Yes. I mean, sure. You can't let just anyone do that. It has to be within a very loving, trusting relationship. Not one that's controlling in an abusive, toxic way. But like, I just freaking love that I don't have to worry about making every single decision in my life, no matter how small or if it's hard. I love that you know me so well that you can take a lot off my plate. It leaves room in my brain to worry about more important things, or to fill that space with much happier things in life. Even just your quick text telling me you'd like me to grab a pack of chicken, two cans of peas, and a Midnight Milky Way on the way home was a huge relief. I didn't even have to figure out what to cook for dinner. Bliss."

If she didn't already make me feel like the king of the world, this little speech would've handed me that title.

Especially when she continues, "You were a hundred percent right. I would've been in my head the whole time we were at the coffee shop, trying to remember every detail of the scenes we've put on publicly at the club—things Crystal and Antonio could've seen me doing, or you did to me. Instead, I got to relax and enjoy the conversation we had with them. So, thank you. You truly are the best partner I could ever do life with, my love."

Her words end in a delighted squeal as I lift her off the ground and spin her around.

"In the words of Frigga, 'The measure of a person, of a hero, is how well they succeed at being who they are.' And you, my little doll, are well on your way to doing just that."

She beams at me, lowering her head to kiss my lips. "Well,

it's because 'At some point, we all have to choose… between what the world wants you to be, and who you are.'"

I groan, moving my arms to where I'm holding her up with handfuls of her luscious ass, hike her up a little higher, and bury my face between her tits, where I growl, "Oh gods—now she's talking nerdy to me? How can I resist her when she quotes Natasha Romanoff?"

CHAPTER 6

Twyla

THE NEXT DAY, I finally do what I've been avoiding since my mortifying misunderstanding two days before. I arrive at Toys for Twats an hour before opening, so I can have some alone time to study the intimacy companion in peace, without having to worry about employees, friends, or family members making me feel awkward.

I'm a scientist, dammit, and I'm curious as hell to check this thing out.

I slowly approach the cardboard box in the back room, which is damn near the size of a coffin. If it weren't for the neon-pink packaging tape and cutesy lettering boasting **SEX DOLL** on the outside, it would give off an eerie vibe. Like at any moment, a long, sharp fingernail could pop through the tape holding the two flaps together and slowly slice down the center, before a vampire stands up out of it, brushing off the Styrofoam peanuts and spotting me across the room—then makes me its next meal.

The image inside my head is terrifying… until a flash of

Crystal as a burlesque-dancing vampiress replaces it, and I smile and shake my head, knowing how badass she must've looked in her costume. I'll have to ask to see a picture at my next lesson this afternoon.

I stand over the box with renewed confidence and eagerness, my box cutter in hand, and bend to slit the tape from end to end. When I open the flaps, I see my imagination was wrong about the packing peanuts. Instead, it's a solid piece of Styrofoam that's been molded to fit the companion perfectly inside the box. The doll looks less real than in the photos, but that's not what matters to me. It's the texture of its "skin" that I've been dying to feel after I read all the scientific details about what they used and the techniques involved to create it.

With a hesitant hand, I find myself biting my lip in anticipation as I use the side of my pointer finger to stroke down the companion's cheek, much like I've always done to my daughter when she's fast asleep.

I gasp and jerk away, unconsciously rubbing the finger with my other hand. "Holy shit," I whisper, and I kneel next to the life-size toy to get a closer look. This time, I trail my fingertips down the nose, then across the shapely lips, which I know can be opened with the remote it comes with. Inside the companion's "vagina," there's a sleeve made of the same material that can be filled with lube and used as a male masturbator. Thankfully, it's easily removeable for sanitation purposes, is reusable, and can be replaced for an extra cost if… overused.

But I don't bother checking all of that. I'm currently stuck on the fact that the toy's lips feel soft and plump, without being too firm, the way a lot of dildos claiming to feel "lifelike" do. I even reach up with my opposite hand to prod at my own full lips at the same time I poke the doll's, and it's astonishing how similar we feel to each other.

I pull back, impressed and mostly satisfied after waiting so long to test the texture. I'm about to stand up and get started on a display for the new inventory, but my eyes catch on the cleavage peeking over the top of the standard schoolgirl uniform featured in so many magazines and pornos. The top three buttons of the white shirt are undone, while the bottom is tied up to show off an unnaturally tiny waist that disappears into a short, green plaid skirt. I bite my lip again, turning to look over my shoulder. Even though I know I'm alone, and should be for the next forty-five minutes, with the front door locked—which would ring a bell if it opened, plus set off a chime here in the back—I can't help but feel like I'm going to get caught if I act on the urge that just filled my head.

I turn back to the companion, which looks like a life-size anime character more than an actual human, and something about its eyes being closed makes me feel safer to act on my urge, but also kind of worse, like I'm taking advantage of it while it's sleeping.

I shake my head at myself. "God, Twy. Don't be stupid. It's not alive. It's just a toy," I remind myself quietly, and with the scientist inside me taking control over the shy and easily embarrassed parts of me, I reach out with a steady hand and cup the top of the companion's breast. The heel of my palm settles into the cleavage while my fingertips land somewhere near the armpit, and I squeeze.

"What the hell?" I say on an exhale, squeezing over and over before shaking the handful, marveling at the wobble of the fake breast. "How the fuck—?"

Again, with my other hand, I reach up my shirt and grope

my own breast to compare. While my boobs are much smaller and real, as in I haven't had a breast augmentation, the companion's chest feels extraordinarily similar to what I assume a boob job would feel like on an actual human. It has everything to do with the texture of the "skin" and its lack of being too firm, as it encloses the silicone implants within.

"You're incredible," I whisper to the toy, removing my hands from both our breasts and standing up. I prop my fists on my hips, looking over the companion with a smile on my face. Not only am I *not* disappointed with the claims the company made about the science and technology that went into making the doll truly feel extremely lifelike, but I'm also excited for others to check her out once I get her displayed in the store. While this toy is more expensive than any other in my shop by several hundred dollars, I have no doubt that once people see and feel for themselves how real it seems, several of these bad boys—er, girls, I guess—will sell.

Eagerly, I bend over to scoop her out of the Styrofoam mold, but I'm surprised to find she's too heavy for me to lift that way. So, I shuffle to the end where the head is, carefully maneuver my fingers beneath the edge of the box, and pull upward. It's a struggle, but I manage to stand it upright, surprised once again by how tall the box and the companion inside it are when I move to stand in front of it. The cardboard is easily a foot taller than me, but the packaging at either end of the doll means the toy itself is probably right around my height. Still, the only other ones of these I've seen in real life were around four feet tall, so this one seems even more lifelike because of its size alone.

With my foot against the bottom of the box to keep it in place, I circle the companion's waist with my hands, rolling my eyes at how narrow this part of it is compared to the boobs and hips, and wiggle everything toward me. As the entire contents comes free, Styrofoam and all, the cardboard falls backward, landing on the floor with a dull thud. I push the packaging backward as well while hugging the toy around her skinny waist, letting out a giggle as I realize the side of my face is pressed to her boobs. I don't know what comes over me, but I turn my face into her cleavage the way Seth always does to me, and…

I motorboat the companion.

I, Twyla Owens, twenty-nine-year-old wife, mother, respected chemical engineer, and businesswoman, shake my head vigorously and blow air through my flapping lips between the silicone breasts of a sex doll.

I laugh out loud as I pull my head back. "If my husband could see me now," I singsong, hobbling backward with the companion until I have her close to the door. She seems steady on her feet, not wobbling at all when I stand to my full height and carefully test the stability with a push and tug of her shoulder, so I let go, take a step back, and fix my glasses that were off-kilter after my momentary psychotic episode.

The skirt on the companion is flipped up, and for a split second, another questionable urge starts to fill my mind, but I shut my curiosity down before the thought can even fully take form. "Too far, Twy. Too far," I say, reaching out to quickly straighten the toy's outfit before turning my back to it and facing my mess.

Walking back over to the empty package, I bend to move the Styrofoam out of the way so I can open the flaps of the box, and when it's clear, I reach for the opening in the cardboard, then pause.

I squint and tilt my head to the side, my mind having caught on the cutesy text printed on the top. The hot-pink tape had come loose from the end the toy's head was at and must've stuck in its current position after gravity did its thing when I had it standing upright.

The tape covers the **X** in **SEX DOLL**, and my eyes narrow further as I try to figure out why my mind is as stuck as the tape is.

And then it hits me. What my eyes can currently read of what's printed on the box is **SE DOLL**. And instead of filling in the correct missing letter, I snort when I realize my brain is trying to replace the **X** with a **TH** instead.

Not **SEX DOLL**.

But **SETH DOLL**.

And like a lot of things that have happened today—without much thought—I hurry over to the desk, snatch up the thick black Sharpie we use to make sale signs, and then squat next to the box as I pull off the cap and stick it on the back end of the marker. I carefully pull the tape off where it stuck, as not to rip the top layer of the cardboard off, and mark out the **X** revealed beneath. Then, I write what my head was begging to see.

Now, on the front of the giant box, it reads **SETH'S DOLL**.

And my heart thuds in my chest as the most brilliant idea for my husband's birthday hits me all at once.

CHAPTER 7

Twyla

"THAT. SOUNDS. *PERFECT!*" Vi exclaims at my idea, who has joined us this time at Crystal's studio. All the kids are hanging out with her husband Corbin, Seth, and the other member of the team and co-owner of the club, Brian. His lovely wife, Clarice, is currently marveling at one of the silver poles, her mouth hanging open as she makes it spin with a push of her finger. Doc is at work, or I'm sure he'd be there soaking in all the uncle time with the guys, since every single one of our children absolutely adore him… just like all us adults do.

"Yeah, sis. He's really going to be blown away. Don't you think, Clarice?" Astrid calls over her shoulder from where we're sitting, legs crisscrossed as we flap them like butterfly wings.

"They fucking spin on their own! All this time, I thought the dancer somehow spun herself around the goddamn pole! My mind… is blown. I am shooketh," she responds instead—something she's been repeating since she first walked in and saw the rest of us playing around on the poles. I even managed to hold myself up for a full revolution without falling.

"We'll take that as a yes," Astrid says, reaching over to squeeze my knee, and we all laugh.

"Now, the question is… how the hell do I pull it off? It's a good idea and all, but I feel like I'm setting myself up for failure. I'm basically going to need an entire personality transplant, or I'm going to look stupid," I confide my worries to the group of women I love most in this world.

Crystal's strong voice makes me sit up straight, like I'm a kid getting in trouble for slouching. "Oh hell nah, girl. Not on my watch. We have… four days to whip you into shape. And dammit, you will, even if I have to bring out an *actual* whip to make it happen. You hear me?"

Her eyebrow arches in an extreme angle, making her look terrifying when combined with *that* look on her normally beautiful face.

"Yes, ma'am," I squeak, then clear my throat, everyone in the room letting out nervous laughter.

Well, except Clarice. While three of us identify as fully submissive, she is perfectly suited for her role as a switch. And instead of nervous laughter, she finally pulls her attention away from the spinning pole to give us all a wicked grin.

"Yaaas, bish," she purrs. "Sic her."

Crystal cackles, scooting to the side to make room in our stretching circle for Clarice, who comes over to plop right next to the intimidating woman. Clearly though, Clarice doesn't find her threatening at all, instead seeming to have found a kindred spirit. They high-five, and then both of them turn their eyes on me at the exact same moment. It's utterly chilling, and I gulp unconsciously.

"So what's the real problem? In order to pull off this surprise, what is the main issue that has you saying you'll need a whole personality change?" Crystal asks, her tone gentling a little.

I consider her question, and while there's quite a few things I'll need to work on, one flaw in particular will be the downfall of the whole present if I can't overcome it.

"I'm a freezer." At everyone's confused look, except for my sister, because she's always known this about me, I prompt, "You know how we've all got that fight-or-flight instinct?" They nod. "Well, there are also two more reactions that aren't as talked about—freeze and fawn. Freezing is my default mode. When I come face-to-face with something stressful, I have a tendency to… get stuck. I don't start swinging fists *or* run away. I'm like a deer caught in headlights. My whole body, including my brain, just shuts down."

Clarice is nodding before I even finish explaining. "I've totally seen this. When I would travel overseas to photograph inside warzones, I saw all three of the responses. It's actually how Brian and I got so close. He was one of the soldiers who fought like hell. Didn't freeze. Didn't run. He got us out of a deadly situation, and with his adrenaline running so high, he didn't realize he'd been hurt. Badly. I didn't leave his side, not even after he finally woke up in medical. He's been stuck with me ever since."

Vi hums. "Mmm… well, maybe on the downlow. We didn't even know about you until a few years ago. And he's been out of the military for almost a decade now."

I've heard this story a few times, so when Clarice says dramatically, "I was his *secret lovaaah*," I know she's mimicking

Karen from the sitcom *Will & Grace,* since my sister showed me the clip after the first time she referenced it.

"So, yeah. I'm a freezer. And when…" I clam up suddenly, realizing I was about to reveal something embarrassing about myself when it comes to my sex life.

"When what?" Crystal urges. "Come on, girl. You're safe here, with us. Not a single one of us is going to think bad of you or make fun of you for anything you confide in us." When she sees I'm still unsure of speaking any more about it, she adds, "And if any of them do, I'll tell their Doms."

All of the other girls gasp at the threat—well… again, all except Clarice, who snorts at the submissives and their reaction. But when Crystal looks her way with a stern expression, even Clarice has the decency—or maybe just the *intelligence,* since anyone could sense the Domme means business—to look put in her place.

She holds up her hands defensively, and says, "I ain't saying shit. My man will jump at *any* opportunity to top. And he's six-foot eight and packs quite the impact."

Crystal goes to turn back my way and say something, but her jaw drops as she gives Clarice a double-take. "Six-foot eight? Goddamn, girl. You can't be more than, what, five-two?"

Clarice gives her a lascivious look, when she replies, "Yup, and before you even have to ask your next question, the answer is *also* yes." She smirks, wiggling her eyebrows.

"Hooo, Lawd!" Crystal hollers, fanning herself before giving Clarice another high-five, and everyone giggles, knowing the two are referring to Brian's… *other* size. Even I do, but nervously, and Crystal notices this detail. "What's the matter, sweet girl?"

When I clam up even more and can't immediately find the words, my sister speaks for me.

"This is part of her freezing issue, or maybe in addition to it. While the rest of us have no problem talking openly about sex and what goes on in our different playrooms, Twy has always been super shy when it comes to those subjects. She told me a few days ago that she's truly bothered by the fact that no matter how long she's worked at the sex shop and spends time with not only her adorably pervy husband but all of us naughty bitches, she never gets used to it." She reaches over and squeezes my knee again, and I'm grateful she told Crystal this in an understanding tone instead of a patronizing one. "I told her it's part of her charm." She shrugs.

Crystal nodded the whole time Astrid was speaking, her eyes shifting between my sister and me, I assume to gauge my reactions to what she was saying. She must've deciphered that I found everything Astrid said accurate. "I can see how that could bother you, Twyla. You see all these girls gossiping and chitchatting about things you might believe should stay private, between you and your Dom, and—"

I shake my head. "No, it's not that. I learn so much just by being around everyone and listening to their stories and casual conversations. I love that they're so open about things. Grateful, even. And I'm jealous that I can't seem to be that way too. It's an unconscious reaction—my embarrassment and clamming up. And you'd think, like… exposure therapy or whatever. I'm around sex stuff all day, every day. But this—" I gesture to my face that is no doubt red. "—never lessens."

She ponders for a moment, her eyes narrowing on me—but I don't think she's actually looking at me—until she seems to come to a conclusion. "Well, until you can figure out a way to *stop* the reaction, we'll just have to teach you how to keep going and not freeze in spite of it."

At my tilted head, she elaborates, "Like, even if you do get that embarrassed feeling, you could find a way to ignore it instead of focusing on it enough that it makes you get all squeamish. So when you feel yourself blush, let that trigger you to make the conscious effort to join the conversation right then, not try to blend into the background. When you get the tight feeling in your throat, clear it out with a loud laugh instead of a quiet, nervous chuckle. I bet that would at least startle you enough to give the embarrassed feeling less power."

She thinks for another few seconds and then nods. "Yeah. That might be it. It's almost like this shameful feeling is its own entity and has power over you. And what you need to do is tell that bastard it doesn't have consent to make you feel that way."

Astrid gasps. "Oh my God, yes, sis! Like Eleanor Roosevelt said—"

I can't help the tears that spring to my eyes as every woman in the room joins in to quote, "'No one can make you feel inferior without your consent.'"

We all squeal and reach for each other, wiggling our fingers at those we can't quite touch. But the moment is broken when my blonde sibling cries out, "Oh em gee! You guys memorized all the words to *The Princess Diaries* too?" and the rest of us burst into genuine laughter.

Even me.

CHAPTER 8

Twyla

I'VE PULLED into our driveway after a much more successful pole-dancing class than yesterday's and see Seth beat me home. He and Luna are playing with her mini basketball hoop in the grass not far from where I park, and they pause only long enough to wave at me. But before I can turn the car off and join them, my phone rings, and I push the button on the steering wheel to answer the call when I see it's Clarice.

"Hey, lady. Everything okay?" I ask, hoping something didn't happen to her on her drive home.

"Hey! Yes, everything is fine. I just thought of something when I let my mind wander on my way to the house, and I figured I'd call and tell you before I squirreled and forgot about it," she explains, and I giggle.

"I get that. What did you think of?" I watch my husband and little girl take turns tossing the miniature plastic basketball through the white-and-blue goal that's half his height, admiring the way Seth's jeans ride low on his hips. His white T-shirt clings to him with sweat, since it's hotter than Hades outside.

"Okay. So. Did you see how everyone straightened up when Crystal threatened to tattle on us to our Doms?"

I smile. "Yep."

"Hey. Don't sound too cocky, there, Twy. You sure did expose your throat to her like a good little puppy when she gotcha for being self-deprecating," she reminds me, and my smile widens.

"True, true. Continue," I prompt.

"Anyway. While I love her idea about using those automatic reactions of yours to trigger you to consciously shut them down, it seems like that would be something that takes time. More time than the few days you have before his birthday."

I nod, even though she can't see me. "I thought the same thing the whole drive home and was praying for a miracle."

She chuckles. "Well, that could happen, I guess. But how about a backup plan?"

I sit up straighter in the driver seat, waving at Seth when he looks over at me with a questioning expression, then give him the universal sign that I'm on a call, with my thumb and pinky pointed outward from my fist as I put it up to my ear. He nods, then turns back to Luna.

"A backup plan would be excellent," I tell Clarice, nearly swooning as I watch the muscles in Seth's back move beneath his thin tee. I'd give anything to be the sub he *deserves*, even if it's just for one night. His birthday.

"Whether you can see it for yourself or not, you are a great submissive, Twy. And before you get to whatever point in a scene that makes you freeze, I know for a fact that you follow your Dom's orders with grace and expertise. I've seen it myself the few times y'all have done a public scene, and when we're just hanging out in general," she says, and as I've been told to do, I attempt to swallow past the lump in my throat that forms when she mentions seeing me *that way*.

My voice cracks like a pubescent boy's when I prompt, "Oh?"

"Yeah. It's more subtle then, of course, but you two live in your roles. You might not address each other by your D/s names or kneel at his feet, but you still do things like look to him when someone asks you a question, keep an eye on his drink and make sure to top him off when he needs a refill, and absolutely glow when he praises you for little things like that. It's a beautiful exchange of power, and your part of that exchange would make any Dominant envious of your man. It seems effortless for you, like you do all of that without much thought, as if it comes as naturally to you as breathing," she explains, and coming from a woman I admire exponentially—not even considering the fact that she's a Domme half the time—it makes my heart feel too big for my chest.

I can't think of anything to say, and it doesn't even have to do with me freezing or clamming up. I'm just... speechless.

But Clarice, being her strongheaded self, goes on without waiting for a response. "So what I'm getting at is you follow your Dom's orders flawlessly, up until the point where you physically can't because of this instinct."

I nod. "Right. And that's the problem. How do I stop the instinct from... being set off?"

"Uh-uh-uh, my friend. That's not your job to figure out. It's your Dom's," she tells me.

My head jerks back. "What?"

"Think about it, Twy. There's a limit inside you, whether you've consciously set it or not. And he's reaching that limit, which sets off your stress reaction to freeze. Other people might be able to call yellow, or red, or their safe word, but it stops *you* in your tracks," she explains, and it rings true.

"Okaaay."

She switches gears. "Let me ask you this. And don't go wigging out. It's important. Okay?"

I take a deep breath, let it out, and make a valiant effort to stay clearheaded when I tell her to go for it.

"What happens during your scene, after you freeze and don't follow Seven's command?"

Instantly, I feel heat creeping up my neck, but instead of allowing my mind to follow its course up the rest of my face, I bulldoze through to answer her quickly, "He recognizes it immediately, stops our scene, and wraps me up for aftercare to let me know I'm not in trouble and he's not mad at me."

She doesn't respond for a moment, and I check my phone to make sure our call didn't disconnect.

"You there?" I finally ask.

"Yeah," she breathes, and I'm surprised by the emotion in my badass friend's voice. "I'm just so fucking proud of you right now, Twy. You did it."

I feel tears try to climb up my throat and tingle my nose at her response, but I laugh to keep them down. "My face is super-hot right now," I admit.

"But you answered me, woman! You didn't let that anxiety steal your voice." After a few seconds—in which she forces me to do a happy dance with her over the phone—she says, "Okay, so that's an excellent Dom. As we all know Seven is. It's a Dominant's job to recognize when their submissive has reached a limit but is, for whatever reason, unable to call their safe word. And whether that safe word is called or not, if a limit is reached, it's their job to either pause or completely end the scene, without any repercussions for the sub. So, just to clarify, he's *always* completely ended the scene? He's never attempted to pause and assess, then continue on with it? Like he would if you called 'yellow' instead of 'red'?"

I nod again. "Right."

"Hm." She's quiet while she deliberates. "Sooo… okay. I think I'm having a thought."

I bark out a laugh, and it must be loud, because Seth glances over at me with a small smile on his face, telling me he heard it even from outside of my car. I snort and cover my mouth when Luna throws the ball at him and nails him right in the crotch. The ball is hollow plastic and way lighter than a normal basketball, but she really chucked it at him, and he falls to his knees in the grass, covering the front of his pants. My face falls right along with him, and I almost end the call and run to check on him. But just as Luna reaches him, she lets out a shriek when he lunges upward and grabs her, pulling her down on top of his belly and tickling the hell out of her.

"What's your thought?" I ask Clarice, hurrying her along now, because I really want to join my little family in all their fun.

"Right. Here's what you do," she tells me.

And hearing her out, knowing she's a part-time Dominant herself, I believe her plan will work brilliantly.

As long as *I* don't mess it up.

CHAPTER 9

Seth

MY BIRTHDAY so far has been one for the books. It started out as a fun-filled morning and afternoon with my girls, exploring the science museum we hadn't been to since before Luna was born. Watching her absorb all the exhibits with looks of fascination and wonder was worth every second of the two-hour drive each way. Now, we're finishing up dinner at Doc's house, where Astrid served the entire crew one of the best home-cooked meals I've ever had.

Even if I'm a meat-eater, and the food was all plant-based.

She made a point to tell my wife each dish's list of naturally grown ingredients every time Twyla or I remarked on how delicious it was, razzing my woman about her undying love for fast food. Well, until Doc shut her down with a laser-focused glance that went from her eyes, to her throat, then back to her eyes. Her little gulp was adorable and so similar to a reaction my wife often has that it makes it obvious the two women are siblings, even while they don't look very much alike.

At the head of the table is Doc in his usual spot, Astrid to his right, with Luna between her and Twyla, since our daughter is obsessed with her aunt. I'm sure it has a lot to do with the fact that Astrid is a professional makeup artist, and they play dress-up every day she's here when Twyla and I are both at work. We would've hired a nanny or at least found a way to split our schedules so she could be with one of her parents at all times, but Astrid put her foot down the very first time she heard what we were considering for childcare. She had finished cosmetology school, now sets her own hours as a makeup artist, and was home "with no one but Scout-boy to keep me company while Neil is at work," so she assigned herself the job of being her niece's nanny.

I'm at the other head of the table—or maybe the ass, unless a table is considered double-headed, like a dildo—as the birthday boy, and to my right is Corbin, with Vi next to him. And finishing out the circle of who I consider my family are Clarice and Brian. At a small table off to the side are Corbin and Vi's kiddos. We tried to get Luna to sit with them to eat, but she insisted she wanted to sit with her daddy for his birthday. Really, I think she just prefers to be around adults when given the choice. She's a little sponge like I was at her age, scary-smart, just like *both* her parents, and although she loves to *play* with other children, when it comes to times when she's not being active and has to sit still, it's the big people she wants to sit with and listen to. Even when there are older kids she could hang out with, she'll choose the adult table every time.

So up until now, conversation has been either PG or *very* coded—since she can already read, so the "spelling things out so she doesn't know what we're saying" phase didn't last long.

She's on her last bite of cake though, so when she swallows, I call her name and tell her to come over to me.

When my little girl is by my side, I lean down and whisper in her ear, "All you kids are done eating now, baby. How about you go claim your spot on the couch for the movie they're putting on?"

She leans around me to peek into the living room, and I look over my shoulder to see what she sees.

Fuck my life.

"It's okay, Daddy. Scout is saving it for me," she says, spinning on her heel to no doubt go back to her seat at the table, but I catch her tiny hand and tug her back to me.

I want to be careful here, because there's no way I want my child to think I don't want her presence. I will never make my baby feel rejected, no matter how desperately I may desire adult-only time. I'm a certified genius. I can figure out a way to get what I want while making sure my little one knows she's always wanted, important, and is not in trouble if Mommy and Daddy need alone time together, as in without her. It's a little more difficult to strategize when we're in a group, because "it's not alone time, since everybody else is here too, Daddy."

While her mama can put her foot down and tell her to go play just "because I said so," there's something inside me that cannot for the life of me turn Luna away without giving her a reason that's acceptable to her.

Maybe it's the years I've now spent as a soft Dom, toeing the line of being a Daddy Dom for my submissive wife. My doll ranks very low on the masochism scale and needs the love, reassurance, and praise that comes with a DD/lg—Daddy Dom/little girl—relationship, but without any of the age regression on her part. And seven years ago, you couldn't have paid me to believe I'd like anything about the DD role, especially if you told me you were taking away ninety-two percent of any type of sadism I could at least enjoy as a consolation prize.

Too much responsibility.

Too much pleasure lost by giving up my sadistic tendencies.

Too much *touching,* and *kissing,* and *cuddling,* and… ugh.

I was way too selfish for that shit.

But then came Twyla.

The twenty-four-year-old woman who'd never even been properly kissed.

And just knowing I was her first everything made me want to be the very best at each physical pleasure and show of affection to be had. I wanted her to experience it all, to never look back after choosing me and ask herself if she made the wrong decision, if she missed out on touches and kisses and cuddles by picking someone who never bestowed those things on anyone he played with in the past.

And seeing and hearing and feeling how much pleasure she got from those touches, kisses, and cuddles, so responsive in a way I'd never experienced before, her reactions became an addiction for me. I began to crave her body's natural response to my every little caress and stroke and gentle squeeze. Became ravenous for her sweet gasps and pretty moans more than the squeals of shock and the screams of begged-for pain I desired from everyone before her.

So *much* more that I don't miss or even think about my former Sadist identity.

That's not who I am anymore. *I* now identify as a soft Dom, and there are no regrets.

So, since that's *who I am,* it would make sense that it carries over into my parenting style. I spend every moment making sure that my wife/sub feels loved, safe, and wanted above all others. Why would I not treat our child the same way? In a totally different way, of course, but with the same result—her feeling cherished like the gift she is and knowing her father will always do everything he possibly can to not let anything bad happen to her.

Or…

Maybe I'm just wrapped around her little finger and spoil her rotten because it physically hurts me when she's sad.

Whatever the reason, my brain knows I probably shouldn't worry so much about her feelings getting a little hurt, and it knows it's a teaching moment I should jump on to make her understand adults just need time away from their kids, and it doesn't mean we love them any less and has nothing to do with them. But my heart can't take it when her sweet baby face expresses disappointment or any other negative emotion.

She looks too much like her mother, I swear. If she looked more like me, maybe I'd be totally different.

But probably not.

I look into her pretty eyes framed by the miniature version of her mom's black plastic glasses and resort to manipulation. "For Daddy's birthday, I want you to hang out on Uncle Neil and Auntie Astrid's couch and cuddle up to Scout-boy, because he looks super lonely over there, keeping your spot saved all by himself. And I really, *really* want you to enjoy a movie with the kids. Can you give me this birthday present? It makes me sad when Scout looks all lonesome. Look at those poor little puppy-dog eyes."

We both glance over at the Australian Shepherd, and since he heard his name, just like I knew he would be, he's looking over at us expectantly.

"See? He's waiting on you to come keep him company. He wants his favorite wittle human," I pile it on.

Finally, she sighs, looks back up at me, then shakes her head while looking skyward, and says, "If that's really what you want for your birthday, Daddy, I guess I'll go over there. You promise you'll be okay without me?"

My heart seizes in my chest while my jaw and fists clench. Luckily, I had let go of her and my hands are just resting on the table. I say through gritted teeth but my voice still steady, "I'll be fine for one movie. But not a moment longer. I'll need my Luna girl by my side after that." I only tell her this because I know she's going to be out like a light for the rest of the night within the first thirty minutes of the show. It happens every time she snuggles Scout.

"Okay, Daddy. Happy birthday," she tells me, before going up on her tiptoes to kiss my cheek and then skipping over to the couch, climbing up to bury herself in Scout's fur.

Teeth still clenched, eyes going wild, nostrils flared, I turn to my wife, who's holding back laughter, and we whisper-yell in unison, "Cuteness aggressiooon!"

After I let out a strangled growl while shaking my fists in the air, I say to the table, "I swear sometimes I just want to squeeze her until she pops or just… I don't know… *bite* her. So fucking cute I can't stand it."

They all laugh, since they were with me the first time I tried to voice what I was feeling when this emotion came over me, before I knew it had a name, and Doc explained it's a pretty common thing. This feeling of contained violence when one sees like… cute puppy videos or adorable babies that just makes them want to *shake* them. According to him, it's just an "involuntary response to being overwhelmed with positive emotions."

Twyla and I have had fun the past four years coming up with different scenarios.

"I just want to punt her like a football."

"I'm gonna squeeze her until her head uncorks like a bottle of champagne."

"I wanna take a chunk out of her fat little baby cheeks."

Things I'm sure if one has never felt cuteness aggression before would make them call CPS if they heard the creative things that have come out of our mouths.

"So, now that you've used mind-fuckery on your own offspring, what's the plan for the rest of the evening?" Brian asks with a smirk, and I very maturely stick my tongue out at him.

Twyla laughs softly. "I keep telling him he's going to have to be stern with her at some point and that she'll get over it, but he just tells me 'that point is not today.' So, until that day comes, I must wear the hat of the bad guy who has the audacity to flat-out tell her no."

She says it with a doting smile on her face as she looks at me, but something about the statement she made doesn't sit well with me. I never looked at it that way, even though I do recall her mentioning how we play good-cop/bad-cop when it comes to our daughter.

It makes me ask myself... have I ever taken the time to consider how my too-gentle parenting affects Twyla and her relationship with our daughter? If I were firmer with Luna, would Twyla feel less like she must always be the disciplinarian?

As my friends carry on the conversation, I wonder...

I wonder if forcing her into that position has been even more stressful for her than it is for other women, since that is in *no way* her personality. While she's an incredible mother who has adapted easily—or at least what I thought was easily until this revelation—being forceful and in charge doesn't come naturally to my tender and quiet-natured wife. So, having to make herself be the "bad cop" toward her own little girl has to… suck. Like, a lot.

Fuck, why am I just now…?

Back in the day—and in what's now considered a twenty-four seven dynamic within the BDSM community known as a '50s household—the wife stayed home with the children, and when they misbehaved to a certain point, all she'd have to say is "just wait until your father gets home." And that was it. She didn't have to be the bad guy. She didn't have to be the disciplinarian. She got to be the *nurturer*, because she'd just tell Daddy what the kids were doing while he was at work or whatever, that they weren't listening to her, and it was *his* job to straighten their asses out.

I just realized… I'm the fucking housewife of our family.

Only, I'm not doing all the other things that were expected of a stay-at-home mom. I'm not the one who keeps the house clean, does all the laundry and shopping, and has a meal ready for my partner to come home to every day. So not only does Twyla do all those things—happily, since she truly revels in her role as a service sub—but she also manages a shop that still to this day makes her uncomfortable. Which she does only because I told her I'd like her to—secretly because I thought it would be good for her to get out of the house, when she seemed like she was slightly losing it being cooped up at home with the baby all the time. *Plus,* she has to be the "mean parent," which goes against… every fiber of my sweet, innocent, and loving wife's being.

I feel like I've been sucker-punched in the balls.

I don't hear anything that's being said in the conversation around me. I'm too ashamed of myself and of the fact that it took me this long to see all this. To see all the stress I've piled onto Twyla's shoulders and hadn't noticed. All the recent anxiety issues she's been having that I figured was normal for any mother of a four-year-old. And her tanking self-esteem.

It's because I've made her be someone she isn't.

I might've changed after meeting and falling in love with Twyla—my past trauma that made me into the sadist I once was so wholly healed that those desires are damn near nonexistent—and be a hundred percent happy about that growth and change. But I recognize I'm still *me*. I'm the same person I've always been, my personality and values and morals still intact.

But that's not the case for Twyla. I've forced her to change at her core level.

And when someone is forced to act against their very nature, of course they're going to feel shitty about themselves, because they're doing tasks and jobs that don't come easily to them. It's hard for them to thrive. It's like taking a cactus, sticking it in a pond, and expecting it to do anything other than what a cactus is going to do—fucking *melt*. It's just not gonna happen, because it's not *built* to handle all that water.

And that's what I've done to my precious wife.

This epiphany, in addition to the conversation I overheard between her and Clarice, are making me question just how good of a Dom I truly am. Our friend was absolutely right when she told Twyla it's *my* duty to assess what's going on when a scene has to be stopped. I should have done it each and every time she froze, had a discussion with her right then and there about what she was feeling, figured out what I specifically said or did that set off her fear instinct, so I could either avoid it in the future or help her overcome it. That's what a *good* Dom would do. Instead, I allowed my emotions attached to *my wife* to get in the way of properly caring for *my sub*.

Again, I can't fucking stand to see either of my girls upset.

And when my doll freezes, she doesn't just turn into a cute little statue. There is a look of absolute fear that fills those beautiful eyes of hers. And for that look to be aimed at *me*?

Intolerable.

Nope. Can't do it.

So, I bundle her up like a baby, and I cuddle and rock her, and I coo sweet nothings and praise into her hair until she's relaxed and blissfully floating off to little space.

While that's great and all for that moment in time, it doesn't solve anything. I'm still a Dom whose sub is experiencing something that should be addressed directly, because it's my responsibility. It is my literal job, my duty, the true obligation of a Dominant who's been given the gift of a submissive of their own, to not only take care of her physically and mentally, but also to never stop guiding her to improve and grow. Not for me but for herself. When I can be successful in that most important duty, *then* my reward will come—because when a service submissive understands their value and believes in themselves and their skills, their confidence will naturally lead them to want to please their Dom even more.

My old, selfish self would find that last part the sole reason to try to "fix" my sub, if I'd owned one back then. Now though, it's an afterthought. My doll, my wife, and her being genuinely happy and thriving in her roles in our shared world is the only thing that truly matters to me.

And that means I need to fix the things I realize now that I fucked up. No excuses. It was all me. I'm the Dominant. She's the sub who did her job of following my lead, like the good girl she is. I led her astray, and now, I'm gonna fucking bring her back to where she should've been all this time. Under the care of a Dom who is fucking worthy of her.

Side note, I should really warn Twyla that phone calls through the car's speakers can be heard loud and clear from outside the vehicle. The cuteness aggression I felt toward my adorable wife when she held up her hand to let me know she was on the phone inside the car a few days ago rivaled all the times I've gotten it around Luna. The only thing that saved her from me going over there, pulling her out of the car, and squeezing her until she squealed was our daughter nailing me in the balls a few minutes later.

And—*fuck my life*—it occurs to me now, I could've easily used that as the perfect opportunity to teach Luna she shouldn't hit boys there just for fun. But instead, I was more worried about making her feel bad that she hurt Daddy, so I played it off entirely, as if my soul hadn't just yeeted itself from my body and left me seeing Tweety Bird for a while after. So convincing, in fact, that even *Twyla* didn't sense the pain I was in—an exponential amount that caused me to miss the plan Clarice and she devised—and that woman is more in tune with me than a damn mind-reader.

Karma, I guess.

Additionally, I'm wondering if I'm doing more harm than good by handling my daughter with… well… kid gloves. What's going to happen to her when she goes to school? She starts Kindergarten in only six more months. Children can be fucking assholes. I know that from lots and lots of experience. Experiences that continued all the way up through college—

never mind the fact that I was almost a decade younger than all my peers. I might've been genius-level book smart, but I didn't have the life experience or the upbringing to know how to recognize manipulative motherfuckers and defend myself against them.

Fuuuck, even I just used manipulation to get Luna to do what I wanted—no matter if it was done specifically to protect her, so she wouldn't get her feelings hurt. Is that just making her more susceptible to it? Will her dad doing that to her, the one man in the entire world she's supposed to be able to trust a hundred percent, make her think that's normal and what people should do to one another? Will it make her weak against coercion when she's older?

Am I doing Luna a disservice by not jumping on every teachable moment I can, to prepare her for life, how sometimes we have to do things just because we're told, because they're the rules, the law? That there are times when she won't be *allowed* to justify her actions or talk her way into or out of things, even when she believes with her whole heart that she's right? What will she go through when she gets into trouble for something I never took the time to teach her is actually a no-no?

And since I'm not doing that, it's fallen on Twyla to try to do all of it, to essentially pick up my slack, on top of trying to be a type of parent she wouldn't choose to be if given the opti—

"Seth!"

My name being yelled in Doc's "Dad voice"—the strong, authoritative tone that makes a kid's ass clench with dread, which, come to think of it, I've never once even come close to using on my daughter—startles me out of my spiraling internal crisis. My ass, in fact, clenching with dread.

When I meet his eyes, his head nudges in the direction of his study. I nod, and we both stand, everyone's stare darting back and forth between the two of us.

No one says a word. No one pokes fun or jokes about me "being in trouble." They know better. They've all been in my exact spot. On multiple occasions. So they know what this feels like. They also know Doc takes his job as our leader extremely serious, and he wouldn't call any one of us out like this unless he felt it important. Especially on one of our birthdays.

The only reaction besides quiet respect comes from my wife. She stands from her seat before I make it past her, places her small hand gently along my bearded jaw, and looks deep into my eyes with so much unconditional love that my chest fills with equal parts comfort and shame. I lean down and kiss the tip of her nose, using my pointer finger to guide her glasses back into place, and give her what I know is a reassuring smile.

All the while thinking, *How could I have done this to the only woman I've ever loved?*

CHAPTER 10

Seth

NORMALLY, I'd sprawl across the couch, fold my hands together on top of my torso, and stare up at the ceiling like patients do in every therapy-session scene ever filmed. But I know Doc's couch in his *home* office is off limits. I know this, because I made the mistake of sitting on it four years ago, and the man threatened me with bodily harm if I didn't remove myself from it immediately.

A threat like that coming from a man as calm-natured as he is intimidating-looking had me hopping up like my ass was on fire, no questions asked.

This is why I trudge directly to the chair across from it and collapse into it, and I watch my best friend take a seat on the couch that shall not be sat upon by anyone but him and his wife. He leans back and rests his ankle on his opposite knee, trying to appear relaxed, but his voice gives him away.

"Wanna vent about whatever it was that had you so spaced

out that you didn't hear me call your name five times before I had to yell?"

"Shrinky voooice," I tell him, but my usual playful tone isn't in it.

"Yeah, yeah. I don't think this is a night you want to waste a bunch of time in here, alone with me, and talking about your feelings. So how about we skip the banter, and you just answer my question?" he counters.

I lift my brow at him. "You know Twyla's surprise, don't you?"

"Of course I do."

While I want to press him for details, a bigger part of me doesn't want to ruin my wife's gift. It's obviously important to her if she's put in so much work to keep it under wraps and sworn our friends to secrecy. She's usually the type who can't keep a gift she's gotten for someone a surprise if it's meant for a birthday or holiday. If she gets it too far in advance, she can't stand the wait and goes ahead and gives it to them. And then she'll feel guilty that she won't have something to give them on the special day, so she gets them something else too. So, if she's actually been able to control herself, then I'm proud of her and will reward her with a genuine reaction. She puts so much thought into anything she ever gets people, especially me. Whatever it is, I'm sure I'll love it.

And I seriously have no idea what it could be. Doc has kept me in the loop about her recent sessions and the progress she's been making, using exercises to build up her self-esteem and learn to have more control over her fear instincts. But as far as the present she either purchased or made for me? No clue.

My only *real* guess, if I piece together little clues from the past week, is she got me a brand-new sex toy that just hit the market, one that hasn't been brought to my attention at the club yet and I would need to educate myself on… with hands-on experience.

That could be why she felt the need to build some extra confidence and try to be able to stop from freezing—this toy intimidates her.

I had another idea pop into my head, but it was too crazy to even entertain. My doll is entirely too possessive—adorably so—to share me with anyone, not even someone who isn't a living, breathing human. So I immediately shut down my harebrained thought that she might be gifting me a threesome with her and the new sex doll she ordered for the shop. And thank God for that, because I would've had to hurt my wife's feelings by telling her I didn't want her present.

Fake or not, I have absolutely zero desire to touch *anyone* other than my beautiful Twyla. That goes for other toys men stick their cocks in to get off. Pocket pussies, cock sleeves, and all the other male masturbators do nothing to pique my interest.

The various parts of Twyla's irresistible body, on the other hand, is a-whole-nother story.

She's all I'll ever need.

"Something my wife said at the table made me realize what a shitty Dom I've been for her," I confess, and my statement surprises Doc. Whether it's because I didn't annoy him into giving me details about the surprise or because of what I said, I can't be sure.

And for once, I've struck him speechless, so I answer the question I know would be his next one.

"What did she say?" My voice lowers. "'I must wear the hat of the bad guy who has the audacity to flat-out tell her no.' And she *wasn't* complaining. She's never nagged me or even done anything more than point out things like 'we play good-cop/bad-cop with our daughter, and I'm always the bad cop.' Not with a pout on her face, mind you, but with an adoring smile. And I'm ashamed to admit that I completely overlooked the things she was *really* trying to tell me."

Doc has come out of his moment of shock, so he's gained the ability to question, "What does any of that have to do with you being a 'shitty Dom'?"

So, I spill everything that went through my head while I sat at the dinner table. Every revelation that branched off into more realizations, I threw it all out there for him to straighten out and organize for himself, so he can do what Doc does better than anyone else I've ever known or heard of. Make sense of things that make no sense, and fix things that seem impossible to fix.

He's nodding, and it feels both good and awful that the conclusions I drew for myself seem to be aligning in his mind too.

He clears his throat before he speaks. "First and foremost, you need to realize you're human, Seth." When my eyebrow arches at him like Dwayne Johnson's once again, while I fight the urge to roll my eyes, he continues. "Yes, Doms have an incredible amount of responsibility, and we're damn-near *expected* to be these all-knowing beings who can predict the future and read minds to a supernatural degree. And *you* an even higher level than that. You have the highest IQ of anyone I've ever met, and you've had that fact shoved down your throat since you were five years old. On top of that, you're known across the world to be one of the top-skilled Dominants in the country, who has been trusted by hundreds of Doms and subs to teach them how to be respectable members of this community."

"Thousands," I correct.

He ignores me and presses forward. "So you've got a battle going on inside you that you may not even realize. On one hand, you've got a *lot* of pressure on your shoulders to live up to what so many people think and say about you. On the other hand, the fact that your reputation *is* so positive and you hear probably every single day what an amazing Dom you are, your confidence in your role is—well-deserved and rightly—high. *But…* You. Are. Human. And as a mere mortal, Seth, no matter how smart and skilled and admired and reputable you are, you're going to make mistakes. Perfection is an impossibility."

What he said about the battle inside me rings true. Only on the outside, I put on a good front that everything I do is done without much brainpower. I'm a genius; therefore, it all comes so easily for me, right?

Wrong. So, so, very wrong.

Yes, I have a brain like a computer, but then God thought he'd add a little bit of spice—in the form of ADHD.

My computer brain has a shit load of tabs open all the fucking time. And most of the time, I think I do a pretty good job of keeping all those tabs organized. But what Doc just said makes me understand that sometimes, a few of those tabs are neglected while I focus more on others.

I feel like my Dom tab has not only been neglected but completely separated into its own window. Out of sight and out of mind.

Doc continues, "Secondly, while you take everything you just told me as something wholly negative, it should also be viewed as a testament that… you're *happy*. You're a man who is truly, genuinely *happily* married and who cherishes the family he's been given. Who *loves* fatherhood and cares about his little girl's feelings so much he avoids hurting them even the tiniest bit.

And you're so happily married, in fact, that your role as a husband who deeply adores his wife has overtaken the other role you have in your life that was formerly the most important to you. The part of yourself that was the 'main character' for so long but has now taken a step back to become a—still highly important to the plot—side character."

I can't help but chuckle at my best friend. "Ya know, I've always admired your ability to come up with metaphors and similes customized for each of your clients."

He smirks, but then carries on when he sees he's getting through to me. "In a *perfect* world for a *perfect* Dom, you'd be able to *perfectly* balance all the side characters inside you. But you aren't *The Office*. You're just a man, brother. And if someone can't forgive that you make human mistakes sometimes, then it's them who's the problem, because they have highly unrealistic expectations." He looks at me pointedly.

"'It's me. Hi. I'm the problem,'" I deadpan.

He rolls his eyes. "You are *not* a Swiftie."

"Not even close. But the radio plays her stuff every-other fucking song, so you learn the lyrics whether you want to or not. At least a couple of them are catchy." I shrug.

"So learn these lyrics whether you want to or not—You. Are. Human," he jabs.

I give him a judgy face. "Um, those aren't the words. It's 'When we're human again....'"

He stares at me blankly after I sing the line, operatically and everything.

After a moment of just staring at each other in a silent game of Chicken, he finally breaks. "Okay, you've stumped me. What the hell are you talking about?"

"*Beauty and the Beast*, bro. Come on!"

His brow furrows. "Astrid watches that with Luna all the time. There's no song in there that sounds like that."

"Duuude. Which release do you have? The 1991 OG version?" I ask.

He pulls out his phone and checks something before he replies, "According to her Favorites list on Roku, it is indeed the one from '91."

"Nah, man. Add the one from 2002 at the earliest. It was the first special edition to include the song that was cut out of the original."

He slowly shakes his head at me. "I'll get right on that."

"Don't shake your head at me. I've already spilled my guts about how obsessed I am with my daughter—"

"Don't say that. It sounds creepy," he interrupts.

"Spilled my guts about how wrapped around my daughter's little finger I am," I correct immediately, because I gave myself the ick as soon as the word 'obsessed' came out of my mouth while being directed at my little girl, when I feel that's the most accurate word to describe what I feel toward my hot-ass wife.

He rolls his eyes. "You were quoting *Beauty and the Beast* for *years* before you even had Luna."

I sink back into the overstuffed leather chair, and just as maturely as sticking my tongue out at Brian earlier, I tell him huffily, "Shut up."

He chuckles, then uncrosses his legs and leans forward, resting his elbows on his wide-spread knees and clasping his hands together between them. "Well… I think your wife is probably getting worried by now that you're spending so much time back here with me instead of at your *big-boy birthday party*," he coos at me.

"Touché," I insert.

"So how about we come up with a temporary solution for your identity crisis to get you through the night, and then we can really work on it when we have more time?"

I sigh and look down. "That feels so wrong to do, when it's something so important. Like we're just sticking a cartoon-covered Band-Aid on a mortal wound."

Doc reaches out and swats the side of my knee, and his voice is gentle when he speaks next. "Seth, I'm telling you, just put it out of your mind as much as you can and *enjoy* the rest of your night. Go along with the surprise without trying to pull hints out of your girl and make her ruin it. Do whatever Twyla has spent the week busting her ass to put together for you. *That* will mean more to her than anything else—getting to *give* you a gift she put her heart and soul into. Even if it's just for tonight, don't try to do anything more or less than you would've before you had your revelation. Just live in the moment of her present. Then you can work on fixing everything else tomorrow."

When I stare at him blankly, he adds, "Doctor's orders," and I roll my eyes.

"Easier said than done," I reply.

"I'm sure. But I have a feeling that whatever happens tonight might just give you all the answers you need."

There's a twinkle in his eye that tells me not to brush off what he's saying. He's not just giving me a careless "it'll be okay." He knows something about Twyla's gift, something important, and it fills me with motivation to swat away the dark cloud that settled over me and get back to the dining room to wrap up dinner and move on to whatever's next in my wife's plan.

CHAPTER 11

Twyla

MY HEART IS RACING as we park in the underground garage, then make our way up the cement steps to ground level. Seth takes my hand as we walk along the sidewalk, pulling it up to his lips to kiss my knuckles as we turn the corner of the building, continuing the few yards until we reach the front entrance of Club Alias. We're here a full hour before the club opens for the night, so we don't worry about masks or hoods to conceal our identities. Instead, Seth uses his key to unlock the door, and when we're inside, he spins the lock once again.

Clarice took care of letting whoever is scheduled to open tonight know that Seth and I would be here and in the middle of a scene when they arrived, so we won't be disturbed inside the private playroom that's been under a little construction today while I kept him distracted at the museum. All I told Seth once we got in the car after saying our goodbyes at Doc's was that our last stop for the night would be Club Alias and to head there right then, so we could get inside and have a little alone time before everyone showed up.

He leads me up the tall, narrow staircase until we reach the top, the sprawling club before us—taking up the whole second story of the building that spans the entire block—in total darkness. Depending on where you're at inside Club Alias, you could be naked and screaming in ecstasy while standing right above the Imperium Security office, Crystal's former workout studio, a fine arts gallery, or a boba shop, and no one below you would ever know, since the whole second level is a hundred percent soundproof.

My heart gallops behind my ribs as Seth reaches over to the pony wall and flips on just enough switches that the public space glows softly. Visible now is the dance floor, the two bars on either side of it, several platforms used during scenes put on by exhibitionists for anyone who wants to watch, and the DJ booth centered on a stage meant for the occasional live musical performance.

Everything is interspersed with tables and chairs, dark and sexy couches upholstered in a material that is both pleasant on the skin but incredibly easy to sanitize and wipe clean between uses, and what seem like random gymnastics mats. That is, until you look way up in the rafters and spot the glinting metal rings that can be lowered and raised with a remote control, which members are able to scan out. Metal rings a willing human's body can be leashed to by a Rigger—the person who does the tying during rope bondage—if they've passed the skills test given by none other than my husband, known only by his Dom name, Seven, inside this sacred space.

And finally, the club's newest additions to the main public area, a few alcoves with rows of spanking benches, St. Andrew's crosses, and what look like pergolas, but instead of being covered in fragrant flowering vines, it's colorful rope that weaves its way through the sturdy wooden beams each night. They were erected for those rope bunnies—the people on the receiving end of riggers' skills—who enjoy something more stationary than what being suspended from one of the rings offers.

Personally, I could just sit curled up on one of the couches all night and watch the couples who play on the rings, and I'd be perfectly content. It's mesmerizing, both the tying of the intricate knots and the interaction between the rigger, also known as a rope top, and their rope bottom. It's so intimate, and yes, makes my temperature rise with embarrassment… but more so, arousal. Knowing they wouldn't be doing it in the main area unless they *wanted* to be watched helps smother the uncomfortable feeling I normally get from seeing something so… sexually charged.

I haven't taken the step of trying it out myself, even though my husband has offered countless times, catching me so often just staring with my mouth hung open while a rope bunny swings high above our heads and contorts their body into whatever positions their specific tie allows. And the times he's snuck up on me while I've been alone, quietly enjoying the show, when he's ordered me to not move as he angles his body so no one can see mine between him and the couch. He knows it would ruin the moment for me otherwise. His hand then wandering up my skirt one night or down my leggings another, until his fingers reach the slickness we both knew he'd find between my thighs.

So much praise. So many words and kisses and caresses of

his approval that I allowed myself to be a voyeur, giving in to my desire to watch those who crave to be watched.

It's all so theatrical, awe-inspiring, and I think maybe one of the reasons I haven't taken him up on it—besides the obvious, that I'm not an exhibitionist, since we could easily try it privately—is because I know I'd never look as cool as them. I'd be too focused on the fact that I might look awkward and stupid, and on top of that, I'd be stuck there, unable to run and hide, even if it were just my beloved Dom observing me.

But I'm on a path of remedying those negative thoughts, and maybe someday I might even have the confidence to be one of those brave souls putting on an arousing show for everyone to see. Until then, I just want to be able to impress one person, one man, the one I belong to, without feeling any sense of hesitation.

And with that thought, the last one of the many that ran through my head in the span of what was a mere glance around the empty club, only seconds after Seth flipped the dim lights on, I reach over and flip one more—the switch to Playroom 2—and he raises an eyebrow at me.

"Okay, so, I need a little time to get ready. So, um… I don't know. Maybe make yourself a drink at the bar or something and set a timer for… ten minutes. Yeah. Ten minutes should be good. If not, I—"

"Take a breath, doll," he interrupts, lifting his hand to stroke along my cheek. I look up into his hazel eyes and do what he instructed. "Whatever you have planned, especially if it takes place here and in Playroom 2, which you know is my favorite, there's no way I won't love it. I'm excited for my surprise, so take as long as you need, and flip the switch inside the room whenever you're ready for me to come in, okay? I'll see the

Occupied light, and I'll give you another minute just in case. Sound good?"

Even though it's *my* surprise for *him*, I'm grateful he knows exactly when I need him to take the lead and pull me in the right direction, making something I hadn't thought about run much more smoothly than what my overloaded mind could come up with on the spot. One of the dumbbells of anxiety rolls off my shoulder, making room for enough relief I can think a little clearer. "Sounds perfect," I whisper, and I close my eyes as he bends down to kiss my forehead.

Then, he spins me around, and I yelp as he slaps my ass to get me moving, making me laugh when he says excitedly, "But hurry up, because I'm dying for my present!"

I shake my head as I make my way around the wall of booths that give the playrooms along the outside of the space a bit of privacy. I tug open one side of the only heavy velvet curtain that's not tied back like the other playrooms', since I asked Corbin and Brian to shut it when they were done, just in case Seth would somehow see what they installed for me today before I was ready. When it falls closed behind me after I step inside, I look up, and there it is—a huge part of my surprise.

I walk over to it hesitantly, taking in the fact that the guys did everything I asked… and more. The room has been rearranged so nothing is within several feet of the brand-new, glistening, golden stripper pole, making it safe for someone to stretch in any direction without knocking into anything. I'd only asked them to install it good enough that I could return home safely to my daughter at the end of the night and to please check the floor when they were done so I wouldn't slip and bust my butt on something.

This, though? The pole looks like it's now a permanent

feature of Playroom 2. And as I round the padded leather play table in the center of the room, I see they even added a thick mat around the bottom. It's black and blends in with the rest of the floor, not a bright color like the ones at Crystal's studio.

Just off the round mat is a black leather armless chair with gold rivets along the edges. It's much nicer than the "metal folding chair or something" I asked them to stick in here for me.

It had been hard enough to request the things I needed, since then they'd know exactly what I'd be doing for their best friend for his birthday. But surprisingly, they didn't laugh or tease me one single bit. They listened intently with thoughtful expressions, nodding as I fumbled through my plan. They smiled encouragingly, prompting me with excitement in their tone and eyes to tell them everything I needed, and they'd get it all done.

I didn't know if their women had warned them to be good, or if the Dominants themselves just sensed I'd benefit from them taking this seriously and that it would help me get through my embarrassment issues if they refrained from giving me a hard time, even if it would've been purely just playfulness.

With my every stuttered request, they'd clap their big hands together and say, "Got it," or they'd ask me if something else might work better. Each of their suggestions was brilliant, and by the time I asked my last favor, my voice was clear, and a smile was spread across my face at Corbin and Brian's enthusiasm. They inserted countless phrases that boosted my confidence, like "He'll fucking love that," and "The lucky bastard," and looking back on the hour I spent with them yesterday, it's a memory I know I'll hold onto and cherish for a long time. Because I know our two normally broody and much-more-serious-than-my-husband friends chose to show me a softer and more sensitive, caring side of themselves, all to *help me* in their own way.

I trail my fingers over the buttery-soft leather of the chair they set up, meant for Seven to sit in and watch the moves I've been practicing with Crystal for the past several days. We didn't have time to come up with anything too crazy or lengthy. Not that I'll ever master anything more advanced than the simple beginner moves that took me days to conquer, when it only took my sister and girlfriends that one hour we spent together at the beginning of the week. But I'm hoping the fact that I'm putting on any sort of performance at all will have him in such a state of shock he won't notice the pole is merely a pretty banister, there for me to hold on to so I don't fall over in the heels I'll be wearing while I essentially just wiggle around a little.

The thought of those heels snaps me to attention. I still need to change into the outfit Astrid helped me pick out and quickly put on the makeup she taught me how to apply to give just the right effect for what I'm about to do. I glance over at the trunk against the wall near the curtain. There's one in each playroom, somewhere for the play partners to store their clothes and other personal belongings while they occupy the room. I hurry over to it, open it up, and pull out the bag that was thankfully left inside for me. I couldn't drop it in there yesterday when I met up with the guys, because someone would most likely use the playroom that night, so I put it behind the bar and asked Dixie, one of our bartenders, to stick it in here after the club shut down.

I close the trunk and set the bag on top of it, carefully removing the makeup pouch and setting it to the side so I can start changing. Quickly, I step out of my flip-flops, shuck my skinny jeans and cotton panties in one move, then tug my shirt over my head as I attempt to yank my feet out of the tight denim around my ankles. In my rush though, I forgot to take off my glasses, and not wanting to break them by forcing the neck of my shirt over them or risking them going flying, I try to reach down to my face buried deep inside the now inside-out material. Unfortunately, my feet just aren't pulling loose from my skinny jeans, and I've basically bound myself with my arms above my head, completely blind, and my equilibrium is being thrown off because my glasses are no longer on my nose, so the world feels like it's tilting.

I'm twisting and turning, growling and grunting, trying to free my top-half and my feet at the same time, and I'm about to truly send myself into a panic attack, because I will absolutely die if my husband has to come freaking rescue me from my own goshdamn clothes like a toddler who hasn't learned to dress herself. When, finally, one foot pops free, knocking me off balance with the sudden loss of resistance, my body spins on the one foot still on the floor, before I topple backward. I scrunch my face and close my eyes, even though I still can't see a darn thing, as I brace for impact.

But a painful crash to the floor never comes. Instead, my butt lands on a soft cushion not even close to the ground. I sit there a moment, assessing the damage to my body in my head, my arms still trapped above me, but other than my heart racing and feeling a little nauseated from not being able to see during all that chaos, everything is fine. Carefully, I reverse the situation with my shirt, setting my glasses down beside me, and then look down at my naked lower half. And I realize I'm sitting on the stack of clothes on top of the trunk—the cushioned seat I landed on instead of the floor.

Thank you, sweet baby Jesus.

I take a deep breath and let it out slowly, forcing myself to undress the rest of the way calmly and with measured movements so nothing else goes wrong. I stand up, turn to face the trunk once more, and glance up into the huge mirror on the wall behind it. When I reach out and touch the glowing button on the right side of the glass, I blink a few times as my eyes adjust to the bright light that now frames the mirror.

I'm flushed from the exertion, my hair wild, but I don't have time to pick apart anything else. I don't want him out there waiting any longer than necessary. I certainly don't want to take so long he comes looking to make sure I'm all right. I practiced getting ready with my sister several times until I was confident I could do a full wardrobe and personality change within fifteen minutes, hoping to cut that time shorter when my adrenaline would be rushing and I didn't have her distracting me.

"You can do this," I whisper to my naked reflection, and with a nod, I look down and grab the cosmetics bag.

First task—contact lenses. I don't want my glasses getting in the way or hindering any position he might want to put me in.

When that's done, and I can see clearly once again, I start on the small bundle of clothes. A sexy pink lace thong, a matching bra that's for absolutely nothing but decoration, a black plaid miniskirt with lines the same pink as my lingerie, a short-sleeved white button-up shirt left unbuttoned but tied in a knot beneath my breasts, and black thigh-high socks with thin pink rings around the tops. An outfit much like the one the intimacy companion was wearing and was conveniently available right at my own store.

Next, my hair. I attempted to learn how to do the French-braided pigtails Astrid first put my hair in when we were deciding on my look, but that was disastrous from the start. I'm just not ambidextrous enough for all that. So instead, we settled for pulling just the top half of my hair back—still in pigtails, but the rest of my hair would hang loose for comfort. When I tried lying down with full pigtails or space buns, it would've taken extra time to get the style just right so my head could still lie flat. If the ponytail holder or bun was even a little too far down or toward the middle, it either pulled my hair uncomfortably or made me look off to one side. I didn't want something as insignificant as a hairstyle to distract me from what really mattered tonight—being the perfect sub.

When my pin-straight dark hair is in perfectly-even half-pigtails, I reach into the cosmetic bag for the style's final touch—pink, fluffy feather pompoms just like the ones Britney Spears wears in her "Baby, One More Time" video. Except instead of scrunchies, these are a smaller version that are attached to clips I easily snap in my hair to hide the two little rubber bands.

I already have on the basic makeup I wore today, which Astrid added to when we got to her house for dinner. There was no way in the world I'd ever master the art of applying false eyelashes, but according to her, they were a must if I really wanted to pull this costume together. And looking in the mirror, I have to admit she was right, as I take a moment to try out a slow blink while keeping the rest of my face frozen.

"Yep. Pretty but definitely creepy. So just right," I murmur, then rummage through the little bag to find the red lipstick Astrid spent quite a while choosing.

According to her, it had to not only be the right shade for my skin tone and hair color, but it also couldn't clash with the light pink throughout my outfit. Even after I reminded her how dim the lighting is in the playrooms, my professional-makeup-artist sister was undeterred. She had to find the perfect red—and red was a must. I agree with her on that part—no other color would do. Red just hits different when it comes to dolling yourself up to… well, pretend you're a sex doll.

At first, I wanted it to be kiss-proof, because I would most likely do a lot of kissing tonight. But again, Astrid had something different in mind.

"Kiss-proof is good when you're gonna be out in public and he doesn't want to be wearing your lipstick on his mouth, talking to people and shit. But for your scene… oh, nay, nay. Nothing will get him harder than watching it smear," she told me with a wink, and the image that put in my head—of the many ways and places he could smear the perfect shade of red—made my face flush to a similar hue.

Again, my big sister had some good advice.

I throw everything back into the cosmetics bag, close my glasses up in the extra case I tossed into my tote last night, and pull out the last part of my getup. The shoes.

I spin around and sit back down on the trunk, setting the pair of sky-high chunky-heeled Mary Janes on the floor before me. I slip my right foot into its shoe, then bend forward to wrestle with the buckle of the T-strap that makes it possible for me to walk in the darn things. We tried basically all the shoes available at Toys for Twats, but every single one made me feel nothing but anxious. So I left those bad boys to the professionals, and we ended up finding these at the mall. They're still taller than any heels I've ever owned in my life, probably twice the height, in fact, but since they're solid blocks instead of stilettos or spikes, I feel much stabler.

Carefully, I stand up straight, then take tiptoed steps in a half circle and a few to the side until I can see myself from head to toe in the LED-lit mirror without the trunk being in my way.

And then…

I smile.

I genuinely smile.

The woman staring back at me might not look exactly like the intimacy companion I felt up at my store, but she does look… sexy as hell.

Aside from the hair, makeup, and schoolgirl attire, the shoes do things for my body I've never seen before. At the mall, I'd been wearing jeans and a T-shirt, and I just made sure the heels fit comfortably enough I could walk and then would be able to dance in them while holding onto the pole. But looking at my reflection in the over-the-top Mary Janes now, I can't help but admire the way my legs look a mile long, especially paired with the thigh-high socks that leave a few inches of skin exposed between the top pink stripe and the bottom of my pleated miniskirt.

I take a couple baby steps to turn to the side, and the shoes have somehow changed my posture. My butt seems like it's been lifted, the hem of the skirt hanging in a way that's a sexy invitation to reach beneath it and grab a handful. My back is arched, and the scientist in me does a quick calculation to figure out it's my body's way of countering the extra height beneath my heels that's higher than that beneath my toes. There's a platform, yes, but my heels are still elevated more than the balls of my feet, which causes my body to naturally situate itself to stay upright. Meaning, booty out and lower back swayed.

And it looks damn good.

My waist may not be as tiny around as the doll's, but the miniskirt's waistband sits right above my belly button, accentuating the smallest part before the pleated fabric gently flares. The two-inch band is tight but not enough to make anything bulge above it, showing just a hint of skin between it and the knotted shirt. When I look down at my body instead of in the reflection, my small breasts look admittedly pretty inside the unlined lace cups of the bra, and I glance up once more, then dip into one of the moves Crystal taught me.

"Oh yeah. Décolletage on point," I say softly, then stand up straight again. "But something is missing." My brow furrows, tilting my head to figure out what the heck I've forgotten. And then it hits me. "Oh shit!" I open the zipper of the inner pocket of my bag and pull out my collar for the evening. This one isn't my official collar, just meant for play, but since the charm from my formal one is on a lobster claw clasp, I was able to attach it the silver ring in the center of this pink-and-black leather choker that buckles at the back of my neck. I adjust it so the circular charm with a numeral 7 in the middle, surrounded by the words Mystical, Wisdom, and Divinity, is centered at my throat.

With a final onceover, I give myself a surprising but confident nod of approval, and then I step back over to the right side of the mirror and touch the glowing button to turn off its bright light.

I turn around and spot the box the intimacy companion was delivered in at my store. It's been set up in the corner of the room beneath the spotlight that's normally shining down on a lockable cage with a mattress on top of it, which was removed for tonight's scene. I've seen it in use a few times. The most startling had been a woman and two men engaged in loud, boisterous sex atop the mattress, while a man who had his penis locked in a little cage of its own kneeled on his spread knees, watching what was happening above him in the mirror now behind me.

After seeing that on a trip to the restroom, since they left the curtain wide open—but hooked the velvet rope across the entryway, which meant they wanted to be watched but not joined—and had a small crowd watching outside the playroom, I returned to the booth our group was hanging out in. I definitely had to have Seven explain what was going on in the scene, then immediately had Doc break down the psychology of it for me, because I just couldn't wrap my head around it. I learned a whole new vocabulary that night, including but not limited to chastity cage, cuckold, hotwife, vixen, and bull.

Instantly understanding that was a kinky path I would never walk in this lifetime.

But I'd never yuck anyone else's yum, so good for them.

Now though, the spotlight is shining down on my redecorated, life-size box. The addition I made in the backroom of my store that changed **SEX DOLL** to **SETH'S DOLL** is still there, now framed in hearts and arrows pointing at it I drew yesterday before I dropped it off at Corbin and Vi's house. And I see Vi must've added silver holographic stickers to make the arrows stand out even more, making them glimmer under the light. It does wonders to draw the eye exactly where I want Seven's when he walks into the playroom. On the other flap of the box, I had written **Happy Birthday** in huge letters from bottom to top, which she also outlined in the shiny stickers.

On the very top of the six-foot tall box is an outrageously large hot-pink bow that perfectly matches the packaging tape I left around the edges. From one of its curled ribbons hangs an oversized card I made him, containing a plastic box that I know will add a little something special for the tech nerd who occupies the same body as an ultra-kinky former sadist.

So there's no way my genius husband will misunderstand the assignment.

Giddy now, still nervous but my excitement surpassing it, I

reach back to the switch on the wall that will turn on the red light outside Playroom 2, indicating it's in use. With the club still mostly dark, I'm positive Seven sees it the second I flip it and starts counting down from sixty. So I hurry as fast but safely as I can in the monstrously high heels over to the cardboard box, opening the flaps, stepping inside, snatching the index card off the interior wall I taped it to, then using the small finger-width holes to pull them closed. Yesterday, I stabbed through the package with scissors when I realized I couldn't pull the darn flaps all the way shut from the inside while I tested if I'd fit with these shoes on. And in this moment, I'm grateful for the height the holes landed—a happy accident that gives me the perfect view of the second my Master enters the room.

His eyes immediately land on the glistening stripper pole, since that's what's straight ahead when one opens the curtain. But seeing I'm not over there, his brow furrows slightly until they come to the corner I'm hidden in. I love that we're here without having to wear masks, because I can see the sexy smirk on his face before he turns and attaches the velvet curtain to the hook on the wall that will ensure it stays shut.

But when he faces inside once again and starts slowly approaching the giant present, my stomach flips, and I fight the urge to burst out of the box and tell him "never mind!" I suddenly feel like prey caught in a trap, watching as a predator prowls toward me licking its chops, even as Seven's mouth stays in its sensual smile.

I can't run. I never fight. So my fear instincts choose what it always does, and I freeze.

But this time, I'm conscious of it. I was counting on it. And I remember this is all part of the plan.

I still sense the fear inside me, the choked feeling petrifying my body in place. Yet with great effort, I take a deep breath and let it out quiet and slow, relaxing just enough to arrange my face into the expression I practiced in my bathroom mirror every chance I got the past few days. With one last glance through the tiny peephole, as my husband—my delicious Dom—comes to stand right in front of the box I'm inside, I then cast my gaze downward, turning myself into the perfectly obedient, respectful submissive I dream to be.

CHAPTER 12

Seven

WHAT THE—?

When I pulled open the curtain just enough to step through, I spotted a new addition to my favorite playroom. A stripper pole, gold instead of the more common chrome, and behind the padded play table in the center of the room, I can make out the top of what must be a chair. The perfect set-up for enjoying a private dance. But one thing is missing.

My tiny dancer.

Out the corner of my eye, something else shiny and glistening beneath a spotlight pulls my attention. It takes a split second for my mind to catch up with what I'm seeing, because for the past decade, a custom-welded cage bed has taken up that corner of this room. But instead, a box nearly as tall as me with a bright pink bow on top is in its place.

My stomach drops to my balls in disappointment, but I school my features, in case Twyla is watching me. My first thought is that she's given me what I feared she might—one of the sex dolls she ordered. She could be hidden somewhere in the room, the dim lighting causing different equipment and apparatuses to cast shadows in all sorts of places in the large space.

As I turn to hook the curtain closed, I glimpse her clothes she had been wearing scattered on the floor, and her toiletries bag and tote are on top of the trunk meant to hold her belongings during a scene. A wicked smile tugs my lips as I think about punishing my little sub for overlooking one of the simplest tasks she's supposed to complete every single time we play. But remembering how nervous and hurried she was before she left my side, I might take it easy on her. This time.

Maybe.

My expression remains though, because the closer I get to the box, the more I sense the woman who owns my soul, and something tells me she's not hiding *behind* the present. Especially when I see one of the flaps make the slightest movement, as if caught in a heavy breath of air.

Everything in me wants to rip it open and see what awaits me inside, but I remember Doc's words. This is important to my wife. She's put so much work and effort into this gift, and that shows just from what I've seen around the playroom.

There's no way she could've installed the new stripper pole herself—not because she isn't capable, but because it wasn't here last night, and I've been with her all day today. Which means she would've had to ask someone, most likely the guys, to do that for her.

A big fucking deal all its own.

There's no way she could've removed the heavy-ass cage bed on her own either. Hell, I can't even move it by myself it's so solidly made. But again, it was still in place last night when I did a walkthrough before I went home to her. She had to ask for multiple things to be done for this evening's surprise, not just a quick request drop and run. And my chest swells with pride, because I know for a fact that wouldn't have been easy for her.

So, instead of diving into the cardboard box, I hold off a moment to take in all the decorations on the outside. Twyla's handwriting up one whole side reads **Happy Birthday!** The thick lines of the black marker are outlined in the same holographic washi tape I remember my bestie Vi using to frame a pricelist sign she made for her table at author events. More so, I remember her telling me the roll of sticky decoration is *called* washi tape, which for some reason I found hilarious.

The same washi tape enhances the drawn arrows on the other closed front flap of the box. They point to a postcard-size label that was stamped in black on the brown cardboard. It's obviously part of the original shipment, **SEX DOLL** in a fun but clearly legible font. But the X has been scribbled through with black marker, replaced to make the label read **SETH'S DOLL** instead, and I grin. Genuinely this time, because God my girl is brilliant.

I have zero doubt she's the one who made that discovery. She has a slight obsession with word searches that began during a hospital stay... which I refuse to think about. It was the one and only time I allowed something bad to happen to the woman who would become my wife, and I don't want to ruin even a moment of this special night with thoughts of *him*.

With my grin unwavering, because I don't miss the tiny holes that could be at eye-level if she's standing on something or up on her tiptoes, I look up at the bow on top, paying its due attention, because I haven't the foggiest where she would've found one this size and with this gaudiness level. Either she ordered it, or she had to buy Hobby Lobby out of their entire stock of hot-pink ribbon, then figure out how to make this thing. That's when I see, hanging from one of the tendrils, is a large envelope.

I reach for it, tugging it free from where the ribbon is tied through a holepunch in one corner, feeling something slightly bulky inside. And then I pull my glasses from the collar of my shirt, slide them on, open up the paper envelope, and wiggle out the folded cardstock to read aloud quietly.

"Seth,

I had no idea what to get you for your birthday this year. I mean, what do you get a man who can snap his fingers, and literally anything he wants will appear... if it's available for same-day delivery?"

I can't help but chuckle at that. It's true. The Zon makes daily deliveries at the Owens residence. I continue reading.

"But then you introduced me to Crystal, and it's like the timing was fated. I might've had a slight breakdown that required the services of our awesome brother-in-law, but as a result, he sent me on a quest. And now, I'm sending you on one too.

Along with this card, you'll find a remote inside the envelope. When you reach each level of the quest, you'll find a card with instructions you'll need the remote for, so keep it in your 'pack' and take it along with you."

• • •

I probably shouldn't, but I can't stop myself. I ask aloud in a British accent, "But what if 'I have too much in my pack already'?" It's a quote our characters say in *Champions of Norrath,* the only video game I've ever gotten her to play with me, and I hear her muffled giggle inside the box before she cuts herself off.

It warms me to my goddamn toes.

"If you noticed, I addressed this to my sweet husband, Seth, and I have one final thing to say to him *and* my master, before Seven fully takes over.

You are the Dom of every submissive's dream. Your instincts and ability to read even the tiniest twitch are nothing short of flawless. You bring me unimaginable pleasure every time you touch me, and there's nothing more I could ask for. Except one thing."

My gut clenches at this. There's something my doll feels she's missing? Something I've failed to provide her as her Dom? Never mind the turmoil from dinner that I tamped down after my talk with Doc—those are mistakes I've made as a husband and as a partner in raising our daughter. This is something else entirely.

I continue reading, my voice keeping its normal tone, so she doesn't feel the need to break character and comfort me, which I know she would if I gave any hint of distress, especially over something she wrote.

• • •

"I am the luckiest woman in the entire universe to be owned by you, and it is my wish to be absolutely everything you could possibly want in a sub."

I go to speak to her, to tell her she is exactly that, but the next line stops me, and I power through.

"I know what you're gonna say. You'll tell me I *am* everything you want in a sub, and you might truly believe that. But I believe I can be better. I want to learn to get past my fears, whatever it is that makes me freeze and unable to obey my master's order. And the only one who can teach me how is you.

So this is my written permission for you to push past my instinctive boundaries."

My throat clicks as I try to swallow, because my mouth has gone dry. Every ounce of liquid has suddenly risen to my tear ducts, making it hard for me to see the words written inside the card.

I manage to blink them back after taking a moment to get control of myself, summoning my Dominant side to take over so I can make it through the rest of this heartfelt gift from my wife without crying like a little bitch.

"If I freeze when you give me a command, I do *not* want you to completely shut down the scene and begin aftercare. Even if

that's what your heart tells you to do because I am your wife and you love me."

Ah, there it is. That's what she meant by the only other thing she could ask for. And she's right. That's something I never would've done unless she specifically asked for it. Even after hearing part of her and Clarice's phone conversation while she sat in her car, I never would've just taken that as a hint and done it on my own. It would've only happened if she voiced or wrote her explicit permission to do so.

I clear my throat and finish reading the letter, because I can't stand waiting to see and touch her any longer.

"I know you are incapable of hurting me. I know that with every fiber of my being. I know that is as true as I do combining hydrogen and oxygen will create water.

And because I know that, and because of your incredible ability to read even the tiniest twitch, as I mentioned above, to know just how far your partner can be pushed, this is also my written oath to my Master, Seven, giving up my right of hard limits. This is the highest gift a submissive can give to their Dominant. A gift not every sub is willing to give, no matter how much they trust their partner or how long they've been together, and something most Doms will never receive in their lifetime. But no one in this world is more deserving than you.

I trust you with my body, mind, and soul even more than I trust my own instincts.

I trust you to push me past where my mind and fears tell me to stop.

I trust you to take my body's natural reaction to freeze the same way you would if a submissive called Yellow, not Red—pause to check in, assess what's going on, and then continue the way you see fit.

I trust in your judgement, to move past that boundary without going too far, but also to take me far enough I'll learn to conquer my mind's control over my body.

I know you'll never abuse the power I'm handing over to you freely, so I have no doubts about giving you this gift. In fact, I would beg you to take it if you're hesitant to accept it. This is not only what I want to give you. This is what I want to give myself. To be a sub who can obey her master's every order without pause, even if fear is still present. I want to be brave.

I love you with everything I am.

Happy birthday.

Love,

Your Doll"

CHAPTER 13

Seven

FOR ONCE IN MY LIFE, I have no words.

There is nothing I can think to say that would be a worthy-enough response to what Twyla just gave me.

So instead of saying anything, I vow to myself that I will give her what she wants in return for a gift I never would have guessed, even if I'd been given a million clues.

Hesitant to accept it?

Fuck no.

But only because my wife has made it perfectly clear this is something she wants. Not only that, but if the past week and all its revelations are anything to go by, it sounds more like something she *needs*. She needs me to take full control and destroy the limits her mind set for her without her consent.

I do need a moment though. To collect my thoughts. To wrap my head around what this will mean for our relationship as Dominant and submissive from this day forward. But only a moment, because I don't want to make her worry.

I step back and prop my ass against the playtable, where I know she can still see me, and read the card once again, this time to myself. It's something I'd normally do, to make sure I take in everything, so it shouldn't cause her alarm.

I accept her gift, without hesitation. But this is a special case. I'm me. And it's Twyla. My wife. My doll. The mother of my child. The woman I'm going to spend the rest of my life with. I'll give her anything she wants, not without thought but because that's something I refuse to fail at. If she needs it, I will stop at nothing until I can provide it for her.

Any other time, a Dom would be smart to hesitate, to really think about what they'd be taking on. I'm fully aware of the power she's handed me. Only an asshole, a fake Dominant who should have no right to call themselves that, would accept the gift of a submissive relinquishing their hard limits, and take it lightly, without respecting what they've been given.

Even in a normal D/s relationship, with limits in place, a Dom should never drop their guard when someone trusts them implicitly to keep them safe. In fact, they shouldn't ever feel perfectly at ease, comfortable to the point of nonchalant, with such responsibility on their shoulders.

Confident, yes. Always confident in their ability. Because a submissive will sense that, and it will aid in building trust.

A sub will also, on the other hand, pick up on it if their Dom's confidence wanes, placing doubt in the submissive's mind, which could turn dangerous.

For example, if I'm confident in my bullwhip capabilities and take great care while wielding it, my doll feels that and can relax, and the whip will feel like a breath against her skin because she doesn't move. If I'm *not* confident, and she senses that, instead of holding perfectly still, she could panic and try to move out of the way but accidently put herself in a position that gets her hurt. Making it harder for her to trust me to keep her safe.

So confidence is extremely important. It's an absolute must.

Cockiness, however, equals carelessness. The last person someone should submit to is a cocky Dom. If a Dominant is arrogant, then they're too self-absorbed to put their submissive's safety above all else. They're too sure of themselves, more worried about boasting than staying unwaveringly cautious.

And that's all with boundaries *intact*.

Take those away....

"With great power comes great responsibility" isn't segregated to just superheroes. So with this even higher level of power to wield—boundary-free, totally unlimited—it's important to be *even more* tuned-in to the smallest of tells, to be able to anticipate not only their most likely reaction, but multiple less likely reactions as well, just in case, before making a move.

So, no, this gift isn't something anyone should flippantly accept; it's not something you can take in then set aside. Some might take offense to the comparison, but it's almost parallel to someone giving you a pet as a present. If you *accept* the new pet, you can't just say "thanks" and then ignore it. You have to *accept* all the work and care that comes along with it. Yes, it's a gift, one that will bring endless amounts of joy, but only if you put in the extensive effort it takes from the moment you agree to the ownership. Otherwise, you're an abusive asshole. Turning it down in the first place would've been the more responsible, respectful thing to do, because it would've meant you put that animal's life and safety at the top of the importance list. If you know you don't have it in you to take on that extra accountability, and you say that up front, then the gift-giver should put emotions aside and see the value in that refusal, because it came from a good place. A boundary that person has set within themselves.

The choice to keep one's boundaries is *always* acceptable.

Any Dom who tries to tell or convince a sub otherwise should spend one night in a submissive's shoes, with no limits, and then see what they have to say about it.

On top of all of that, there's something else a Dominant must consider before accepting this gift.

There's already a battle we fight within ourselves, as Dominants, to follow all the rules set within a D/s relationship. Like it or not, that is a *choice* we make each and every time we put our hands on our subs.

We are human, after all, as Doc likes to remind me.

It would be so easy to let hormones, selfish pleasure, and animalistic instincts rule, to keep going after someone who's at your mercy tells you to stop—as in they truly want you to quit what you're doing to them. It's an ugly reality, but it's reality nonetheless.

That battle is easily won for some, barely even a whisper of a thought that passes through one's mind—after all, you can't make the decision to follow a rule if you aren't conscious of there being one. You can't make the right choice if the choices aren't presented. The millisecond it takes for your brain to pose *"Rule 23. Follow? Yes/No"* and then the millisecond it takes to decide *"Yes"* could be the whole of it, the entire battle taking place within less than a second. But it's still a decision that was made, no matter how quickly.

For me, the agreements we've made set the scene itself. I'm aware of what she likes and doesn't like, so why would I include something I know she doesn't enjoy? But while playing, experimenting, trying something new, or maybe something old but in a different way, we might stumble upon an act that toes a boundary.

As her Dom, it's my job to recognize it. It's my duty to stay behind it, even if she seems like she's enjoying what we're doing in that moment. Limits are not to be broken unless that's discussed before the scene begins. Period. So, I make the conscious decision to not go past it.

I never would. For me, it's a battle easily won.

But it's still a choice I make.

Then there are Doms, *good ones,* whose battle isn't so simple. They have to put in a tremendous amount of effort to make the right choice, to adhere to their sub's limits. They can make the right decision every… single… time, never once crossing that line, yet internally, they've gotta beat back that beast with every ounce of self-control within themselves.

That's a case in which a Dominant should most definitely hesitate before accepting their partner's unlimited submission. To ask themselves some important questions. Like, with no boundaries to be conscious of, no guidelines, would they have the ability to focus on not pushing their submissive too far, if they already have to put so much of their willpower into not pushing them past things they've made it clear they don't want to do?

But on the other hand, some people naturally want to rebel against rules, and that's where that struggle trying to play within them comes from. They just hate coloring inside the lines and want to let their creativity roam free. Hand them a drawing pad instead of a coloring book, and they're perfectly content and will create something beautiful.

So in *that* Dom's case, removing the rules might ease some of that instinctive opposition, taking away the pressure to conform. Making them more trustworthy without boundaries than they were with them.

There are so many variables. So many things to consider. It would be a sign of wisdom for a Dom to take their time making such an important decision.

But for me, the decision was made the moment she wrote these words. Because I will deny her nothing. And if taking on this extra, tremendously imperative responsibility is what she needs me to do, then goddammit, that's what I'm going to do.

And I'm going to relish every fucking second of it.

CHAPTER 14

Twyla

WHY ISN'T *he saying anything?*

Why isn't he ripping open this box and having his way with me?

I blink my eyes into focus, after holding the doll-like expression in anticipation of him opening the flaps and getting his first look at me, and I peek through the little holes to see what's going on. He's reading the card again, his face stoic, and instead of panicking that I gave him a shitty gift, the expression soothes me.

He's taking what I wrote seriously. He's reading the words again, silently this time, to better absorb them, to mull them over in his mind. And any time he does this, the results are always astonishing. Usually it's him reading the instruction manual for something.

Yes, I'm lucky enough to be married to the only man in the world who actually makes a point to read the instructions from front to back.

But it's after that the magic happens. Along with his genius-level IQ, he has a photographic memory. Reading that instruction manual all the way through, it's now saved inside his computer mind as if his eyes were a scanner. And he can put whatever it is together without glancing at the directions ever again.

And he's doing that same thing with the card I made him.

So I force myself to relax and wait patiently for him to do his thing.

Because I know when he's done…

Magic will happen once again.

CHAPTER 15

Seven

TAKING HOLD OF THE REMOTE, I slide the card back inside the envelope and walk over to the trunk to set it next to my doll's things. I use the time it takes to close the distance between us to let this side of me fully override my being.

Since I met Twyla, the part of me known as Seven hasn't come out to play, not completely. Those sadistic urges that were once the entree of my sexual appetite have barely registered as an a la carte side dish for the past several years, a different craving—one focused on bringing overwhelming pleasure to the woman I love—taking over as the main meal.

But along with that, other parts of my domination have softened. Too much so. Everything I've heard and read and learned today has shown me that, loud and clear. And while I've enjoyed living in this gentler embodiment—so much I could live the rest of my life this way and never feel like it's lacking—a larger, deeper part of me is making itself known. Unfurling.

Stretching its legs. Cracking its stiff joints back into working order.

I can't help but acknowledge that I feel more like myself in this moment than I have in years.

And it has nothing to do with sadism.

Gone are those urges. Possibly forever. Since sadism means one gains sexual pleasure from the act of inflicting pain on another person, I can say with complete certainty that I am no longer a sadist. I'm downright allergic to the idea of hurting my little doll.

But what I've been since becoming a husband and father was *not* Seven-minus-sadism. The Dominant I've been has lacked far more than that. I also haven't been a disciplinarian. I haven't been a teacher who pushes his pupil to *excel* rather than merely pass the course. I haven't demanded… ruled… *dominated* my submissive. My commands have been more like suggestions. My orders more like requests.

But I'm not disappointed in myself when it comes to this change. When our relationship began, Twyla was a virgin. In fact, she was innocent in more ways than just being sexually untouched. BDSM was a whole new world to her, one that would've blown her mind to the point of refusing to understand it and running far, far away had she not been such an intelligent and adaptable person. And the second my soul recognized hers as its other half, my whole Seven persona had to become adaptable as well—something it had never needed to be before.

Because if Vanillas were in one hand and Kinksters in the other, Twyla would've been sitting up on the shoulder, looking down at everyone and asking what the fuck they were talking about. To my sheltered doll, vanilla was just an ice-cream flavor, and kink had something to do with curly hair.

So without doing it on purpose, and without much internal pushback, I slid down that scale from Dominant to Vanilla like my ass was on a three-story staircase banister, my balls slamming into a pineapple-shaped decorative finial somewhere around the halfway mark.

In other words, if my Dominant side were an HVAC system, I dialed the heat *aaall* the way back to Low, to the degree right before the cold air would kick on.

In other words, I was one step away from becoming just a dude who liked enthusiastic lovemaking that included teammates.

Teammates being toys. Because only insecure little fuckboys see toys as intimidating, instead of a way to bring their woman even more pleasure than one mere mortal can deliver on his own.

But this mere mortal has finally realized that my sweet, innocent submissive wife no longer needs a Level One Dom. In fact, after what she wrote in her card, she needs a far more advanced Dominant than even the kinkiest, most sadist motherfucker this lifestyle has ever seen.

She needs a Dom worthy of a sub with no limits.

She needs Seven.

The *real* Seven.

The one who's not *lacking* past roles but who's focusing on the ones his submissive needs most.

I'm not old Seven minus sadism.

I'm Seven—the old one, plus a heart.

And that heart stands inside a cardboard box only a foot away.

I smirk, reading over the words written on the right flap. "***Seth's* Doll**, hmm?" I purr, reaching up and using my pointer finger to trace an X over the name. "Well… I hope he doesn't mind sharing his birthday present, because it's my birthday too."

A rebirth. A new and improved Seven just for you, doll.

I'm so close to her I can hear Twyla's gulp, and I feel my cock come to life.

Without making her wait a second longer, I press my knuckles against the left side of the slit, which makes enough room for my fingers to then slide beneath the right, and slowly, I open my most precious gift as a Dom.

I hold my breath, the light from overhead spilling in, giving me my first look at the beautiful woman inside as I open the other flap. And for the second time tonight, I'm speechless.

Gone is my wife, the girl other people always describe as pretty and cute on most days, and lovely when she's here at Club Alias. In her place stands a version of her I've never imagined. The fact that I've never felt the urge to imagine her as anything but her authentic self is besides the point, because I don't think I could've pictured the woman before me even if I had.

And all woman, she is, even dressed as a sinful schoolgirl who would be sent straight to the headmaster's office for every dress-code violation in the handbook. On top of all that, she holds perfectly still except for the movement of her breasts as she breathes and her throat as she swallows nervously. Her eyes are focused on my chest, which would be directly straight ahead if she were at her normal height, but in these shoes that are straight out of an anime nerd's wet dream, it means her gaze is lowered.

My good little sub.

Her painted-red lips I'm already considering how to smear

are slightly parted, but I can see her jaw is tightly clenched to keep her features from moving, and I'm impressed as hell by her commitment to this role she's playing. She's not normally one who can allow herself to dramatically portray some character, too worried she'll look silly or isn't doing it right. The only time none of that seems to enter her mind is when she's playing pretend with our daughter.

But right now, I've been staring at her for quite some time, and she's only blinked once, purposefully, a *slow* blink that made her cosmetically enhanced lashes appear just like a doll's would as she kept that faraway look in her eyes.

My cock hardens further.

Trailing my gaze downward, I see she's holding an index card, the thick paper slightly trembling between her fingers, and instead of my usual compulsion to soothe her nerves, I allow myself to latch on to that dark pleasure I always felt before I met my wife. The power one feels knowing your presence alone, the anticipation of what you might do next, without ever having touched them, makes them have an outward physical reaction.

I have to reach down and adjust my cock inside my boxer briefs, worried it might break through the fucking metal zipper of my jeans I'm so hard. And when I glance up at my doll's face, the pink she added to her cheeks this morning with a brush has spread but through her blood vessels.

There's my girl.

I lift my hand and use the side of my knuckle to gently caress her cheek, her lashes fluttering before she catches herself. "It even blushes? Wow. How lucky am I? That's always been my *favorite* feature of my own doll," I say, letting that hang in the air for a moment so she can absorb it fully. She hates that she has no control over her sensitive nervous system, but my God, I've always gotten off on it. "I never have to wonder if she's hiding something inside her. I can always tell just by that pretty blush she can't control."

I lean in like I'm telling her a secret, when I whisper, "You see, she seems to believe it's all me, that I'm just that good at reading *anyone's* microreactions. And while I'm admittedly pretty damn talented when it comes to that, it's actually *her* that makes it easy for me." I lean even closer, inhaling deeply as I run the tip of my nose from her collarbone to her ear, making her shiver. "If it weren't for *my* doll's involuntary responses, I wouldn't be nearly as good at overwhelming her with pleasure."

My tongue slips out to toy with just her huggy-hoop-impaled earlobe, and I hear her small whimper just before I feel a sharp jab against my abs. I grin but hide it before pulling back and looking down, seeing she's holding the card out toward me, her finger still pointed after poking me, and when I lift my eyes to hers, they're back to the faraway stare.

Again, I'm so fucking impressed with her refusal to break character.

"Oh, what's this?" I ask like I hadn't noticed the index card before. I take it, once more pulling my glasses from my collar, and read the first note.

"**Hi, I'm your brand-new intimacy companion! I've been updated and much improved since the model before me, and I hope you enjoy my new features.**" I swallow the lump that wants to form in my throat at the idea my wife felt she wasn't good enough exactly as she's always been. There's no room for that here, in this moment, so I shove that part of me back down and give Seven extra strength to keep it at bay. "**If you push the pink button on my remote, it will activate Test Mode One.**

This mode is a safety feature to make sure all my parts are in working order BEFORE you play with me. Please do not skip this step. Watch carefully but from a distance of at least four feet. If you notice any of my body parts not bending or moving in a natural way or if you see or smell something burning, the red button is the emergency stop. Contact the number on my box for troubleshooting help. Sorry, no refunds."

I chuckle as I take my glasses back off and hook them in their usual spot at my throat when I'm not wearing them. As if I weren't impressed enough, the thought and wit she put into the note brings my pride to a whole new level, and I find myself looking forward to not only what she's going to do with each press of a different button, but also what the next index card will say.

"I don't know how I feel about taking orders, especially from an inanimate object," I speak coolly. "But I'm curious enough about what you'll do once you're no longer inanimate to put those unidentified feelings aside."

I make a show of looking over the black remote, which is a simple thing, about the size and shape of our smart TV's, only it has a single line of different-colored buttons down the center. I recognize it as a universal remote you can set up much like voice commands and routines on an Alexa, each button doing whatever you've programmed it to do.

So fucking brilliant, my girl is. The perfect tool to help keep up the sex-doll façade.

"Pink for Test Mode One," I repeat the instructions, and without further ado, my finger presses the button at the top.

My head whips around toward the new stripper pole as a disco ball lowers from the ceiling near it, a bright light coming on to shine direct at it as the rest of the lights in the playroom dim. I'm taking everything in, the shimmers produced from reflecting off the mosaic of mirrors mesmerizing, so I miss her stepping out of the box, but I feel her nails through my shirt as she lightly drags her fingers from my right shoulder across my back to my left as she passes behind me.

I don't move, frozen to the spot, the remote still lifted while I watch slack-jawed as this woman I hardly recognize sashays toward the pole. Her hips move in a way that's nearly hypnotic as she takes long strides that had to have been practiced in those shoes. The skin between her thigh-high socks and the pleated skirt peeks out more with each step, and it's the perfect level of tantalizing, making me crave to peep underneath.

She comes to a stop next to the new leather chair, her back still to me, one leg locking while the other snaps against it, slightly bent as the heel of the shoe hovers an inch off the floor. Her left hand props on her left hip, and suddenly her right arm lifts straight up in the air, her finger pointing skyward. And like magic... or impeccably planned timing on her part... music begins to thump around us, and I immediately recognize it as "Lick" by Joi featuring Sleepy Brown, a song off the *XXX* soundtrack Twyla added to her playlist when we had a Vin Diesel movie marathon a couple of years ago.

My eyebrow cocks when her position holds but her finger that had been pointing straight up suddenly snaps downward on beat with the bass. She turns just enough to peek at me over her shoulder, and I follow her silent command, but only because I'm allowing my wife to give me her gift. When I start to head toward the chair she pointed me to, she faces forward once again and continues on her way to the pole.

My eyes never leave her as I lower into the buttery leather

seat, holding my breath as she steps from solid floor to the black mat surrounding the base of the pole like a tree skirt, but she manages it flawlessly. And the air then leaves my lungs in a long exhale through pursed lips as she grasps the golden apparatus in her right hand, hooks her right ankle at the bottom, leans all the way out from it, then seems to fall forward. But because the whole thing spins on its own, the movement is nothing but sensual grace as she swings around to the front, now facing me, before letting go and putting her back against the metal.

Then Joi starts to sing. *"I lose all control…"*

My doll cups her breasts, then slides her hands up her chest, her neck, into her hair…

And just as the words *"when you grab ahold…"* are heard, she lifts her arms to grasp the pole above her head with both hands, making me wish it was my cock instead. Or my own hands around her throat.

"And you do your trick…"

She holds herself up with her two-handed grip, and in a precisely equal move, her legs part wide.

"I love it when you…"

At the exact moment Joi sings the final word of the stanza—*"lick."*—my doll slides straight down the pole, and if I didn't have such a tight rein on each of my personalities, I would've probably whimpered the effect is so fucking sexy.

She knew damn well while she was creating it that I'd read into every second of this performance. And with her legs now spread obscenely wide, her thighs completely exposed as her tiny skirt hides nothing but her pussy in this half-squatted pose, that repeated word—*lick*—hits me right in the dick. Because all I'm thinking about now is doing exactly that.

I don't hear it over the music, but I can feel the plastic remote groan in my hand as my grip tightens unconsciously. Not wanting to ruin the surprises in store for me or the work she put into them, I reach over without peeling my eyes away from my little dancer and set the remote on a rolling tray table I know is next to me.

It's a good thing too, because that's when she starts rolling her hips to the sensual beat, and I feel my cock jerk, surely soaking the front of my boxer briefs with precum.

She stands back up in one fluid motion, her legs sliding back together, then takes one hand off the pole above her head to trail it from one side of her throat to the other beneath her black-and-pink collar as Joi sings, "*You've got lock and key…*" Replacing her hand where it was, spinning to give me her back, and lowering her grip down the pole as she steps away from it enough to bend all the way forward until her upper half is perfectly flat, she hits this pose just as "*Every part of me…*" fills my ears.

Meaning I own everything she's showing me.

The part of her body I can finally see beneath that black-and-pink-plaid miniskirt.

The rotating disco ball reflects the spotlight just right for me to catch a glimpse of the pink thong she's wearing, and she's bent so far forward it's not just lace disappearing between her cheeks. It's *all* of that thin material that's visible, the part that's usually concealed by the rounded globes of her ass, plus the other few inches that has her perfect pussy hidden behind it.

Somehow, the fact that I can see that little pink thong all the way from back to front is more arousing than if she'd bent over and revealed she was pantiless.

If there's hidden meaning to decode between the rest of the chorus and her movements, it's lost on me, because my mind focuses solely on the erotic vision she creates as she continues to dance for me.

By the time she turns to face me once again, I'm so aroused I can barely stand it. And that's when it dawns on me, I'm not in some strip club with rules to follow. I'm in my own goddamn sex club, with my own tiny dancer who wants nothing more than to please me.

So, I stand up from the chair at a gradual speed, as not to startle her and make her stop her performance. I'm rewarded for the forethought, because instead of faltering, her eyes focus on my hands as she keeps going, the reflected light exposing the flush taking over her beautiful face while she watches me undo my belt, then slide it slowly from its loops. Unconsciously, my movements as I fold the leather, grip it in one hand, and unbutton my jeans match the beat of the music along with her, and the tension building in the space between us makes my heart pick up its pace. Especially when her extra-long lashes make it obvious when her gaze follows my fingers as I lower my zipper.

I don't take off my pants, because she might have a plan for getting me out of them, so I pull my phone and wallet from my pockets and take a seat once again, placing the items on the tray next to the remote. Resting the belt across my lap, my eyes never leave her once in the time between bending forward to untie my shoes and tossing them and my socks beneath the rolling tray table. And thank God for that, because it's in those moments she lets go of the pole to untie the knot of her shirt just beneath her breasts.

I'm vaguely aware of the lyrics saying something about not making her wait much longer, as the shirt disappears from her body, and a bra remains that I'd bet every dollar to my name perfectly matches the little pink thong beneath her skirt.

A smirk on my doll's red lips draws my attention away from her pretty tits, making me realize my arm is still outstretching in midair from when I tossed my shoes. My eyebrow lifts at her expression, and I know she spots the warning when I see her gulp before schooling her features back to her doll-like appearance. If she hadn't, I'm sure my hand slowly coming back to my lap to grip my doubled leather belt would've straightened her out.

The next thing to go is the pleated skirt, which leaves her curvy hips mid-spin as she hooks her right leg around the pole while gripping the metal with her right hand, using the left to release the Velcroed strap at her waistband. When she remains in nothing but her matching set, thigh-high socks, and those sinful Mary Janes, it takes everything in me not to charge forward out of my chair and detach her from the pole to make her ride mine instead. But at the same time, I'm frozen in place, enchanted by the confidence pouring off my doll as her left hand joins her right, her body turning as she unhooks her leg and repositions so that both thighs come up and cross to clamp around the golden pole.

She pulls herself closer as she continues to spin, arching and throwing her head back, which causes her ass to become the main focus of the show until it vanishes from view for half the rotation, making me a salivating and panting fiend inside as I anticipate its reappearance.

I'm watching that ass so closely, then making my own plans inside my head for that part of her, that she's already stepping in my direction before I even realize she's come down off the pole. And then I get to watch that sensual walk from earlier, only this time from the front, made even more erotic as my eyes train on the redness along her inner thighs as she approaches.

Can't say I've ever been jealous of a stripper pole before.

I want to be the one to cause her flesh to turn red.

And not just from making her blush.

Her eyes are focused on the floor between us as she takes her careful but graceful steps, but the moment she's directly in front of me, so close I can feel her body heat along my spread knees, her expression shifts back into its doll-like state. It makes me wonder if concentrating on keeping that countenance is helping keep her nerves at bay, if that's the practice she's using to accomplish this goal of hers, this exceptional gift she's giving me. If so, I could use that—*we* could use that—to aid in her quest to become the sub *she* wants to be.

I'm pulled out of my thoughts as my doll bends forward and picks my belt up off my lap, obviously thinking on her feet as she gently places it behind my neck and pulls the ends over my shoulders like a scarf. I allow it, since my taking it off wasn't part of her carefully laid plan, and there's no way for her to ask permission without breaking character.

I can actually see it in the miniscule nods of her head and tiny twitches of her lips that she's counting the beat of the music, trying to quickly figure out where in her choreography she should be, since I messed it up. But before the feeling of guilt can sneak up on me, it's deflected with that earlier sense of pride as my doll picks up her dance flawlessly, her next movement placing her at my right side until she lifts her leg over my lap, then slowly takes a seat.

I can feel how hot her pussy is through the material between us, letting me know she hasn't compartmentalized so thoroughly that this scene isn't having an effect on her. The knowledge that it *is* thrills me to no end. But I hold perfectly still so I don't disrupt her again. There will come a time in the future when I'll allow myself to enjoy purposely fucking with her to see how she handles it. When I'll have fun coming up with rewards and punishments for her reactions to the wrenches I throw her. Right now though, the best and most important thing I could possibly do is stick with *her* plan. Do all I can to make sure everything goes according to what she's designed for this evening.

She places her hands on my shoulders and begins a lap dance so erotic I'm thrown back in time, feelings coming over me I haven't felt since I was in college. I was so many years younger than my peers but living in the same dorm, exposed to partying and sex, the walls practically drenched in hormones. But it's not the anger and hurt that came after all of it that my memory is conjuring. It's the excitement and adrenaline rush from experiencing something so fucking new and delicious you believe it'll never get old.

This dance is so fucking hot it's like experiencing my *first* lap dance all over again.

Which is saying something, because I was barely past puberty at that point and could've come in my pants just by someone even glancing in the direction of my dick.

And the excitement only grows from there as my doll removes her bra, then veers from her original choreography—since she grasps hold of my leather belt on either side of my neck, which technically shouldn't be there—and stands so that my face is level with her bare breasts. And then she tugs me toward her, her elbows pressing her small tits together to cushion the impact, and I swear to God I nearly drool right down between them as my mouth lands in her cleavage.

It has me questioning if I'll be making fun of Brian for being a switch *ever* again.

She sits back down on my thighs, stealing her softness from where I'd happily suffocate, but keeps hold of her leather reins, and I tense the muscles of my neck and back to give her the stability she needs in order to complete her next gloriously erotic move. She throws her head back, her spine arching until her hardened nipples are pointed at the ceiling, and then dips even farther, to where all I can see from this angle is the underside of her chin, past and between her breasts.

I can't help it then. I cannot and will not control the overwhelming need I feel in that moment to taste my little doll. And so I slide my arm beneath her arched back to hold her right above her hips, keeping her steady as I lean forward, her grip on the belt no longer needed as I take her weight and—right as the singers groan *"Lick"* once more—swipe my tongue from her belly button all the way up to the center of her chest.

She shudders, her upper arms squeezing her tits together once again, and I devour the flesh of her cleavage, sucking the soft skin and firm meat beneath it into my mouth to the point I get what I wanted. I'm now the one causing the red marks along her pale flesh, and her whimper and corresponding tug on the belt around the back of my neck only makes me suck harder.

See, little doll? I'm not a psychic. It's your body that tells me exactly what it wants, I think but don't say, because I've already deviated from her plan enough. I need to take back control over my own desires so she can see this night through the way she wanted it.

I unlatch from her breast, my pulse now thumping inside my cock while I take in the angry marks I've left behind as I sit up. I wait for the feeling of regret I normally get on the rare occasion I bruise my wife's flawless skin, but it never comes. Especially as she stays in this position draped over my arm, her ribs making faint appearances with each deep inhale as she catches her breath. It wasn't the exertion of her dancing that caused her to start panting like she just ran a marathon. Her breaths were mostly even when she first perched her soft ass just beneath my cock. No, this is all me.

This is all thanks to the Dom she now needs and craves—one who will handle her like a beloved fuck toy instead of a porcelain baby doll or fragile figurine.

CHAPTER 16

Seven

WHEN HER CHEST is no longer heaving and I feel her start to try to sit upright, I move my arm to where my hand slides up her spine, then into her hair to cup the back of her head, my forearm still along the middle of her back as I lift her with ease. It brings the front of her body flush with mine, and I hold her there for a long moment, enjoying the intoxicating eye contact between us.

The song coming to an end brings her back to the present and her task at hand far too quickly, and almost immediately, she gives me an erotically creepy slow blink that signals she's back in character. Reluctantly, I drop my arm, allowing her to lean back a little as she lets go of the belt she's been clinging to like a lifeline. She flexes her fingers a few times, and I hear them crack. I smirk to myself, knowing I'm the reason her grip had been so tight on the leather strap.

Reaching around my shoulder, her hand reappears between us a second later holding an index card I hadn't noticed taped to the side of my chair, since I'd been unable to pull my eyes away from my dancing sex doll for longer than it took to blink.

I look back up at her eyes, the faraway look in place, but when I don't immediately take the card from her, I catch her take the quickest glance at my face, making one corner of my lips tilt up when she realizes she'd been seen. Yet she's back to impressing the fuck out of me with her performance when instead of pouting or reacting in any other way a lifeless plaything wouldn't, she slow-blinks twice…

Then robotically lifts the index card between our faces.

And although I'm still fully embodied by the Dominant inside me, neither of my personalities can resist it.

I toss my head back and laugh.

"Perfection," I say when my laughter subsides, and as I take the card from her hand, unblocking her face from view, I catch the flutter of her eyelashes at my praise. "Now, let's see."

Just then, the disco ball and its spotlight lift to their original spot, and the lights of the playroom brighten to their usual ambiance.

"Let there be light," I murmur in awe. She had thought of fucking everything, right down to bringing the lights back up so I could read the next card. Which I do once I don my reading glasses.

"**If Test One has been completed to your satisfaction, it is now time to move on to Test Mode Two. While the first test was to check that all my limbs and joints and my outer features work properly, this second test is to do the same for my internal features. One of these include my built-in lubrication system—**" My lips stretch into a smile, but I manage to keep from laughing at how clever this is. "**—which should automatically coat two out of my three pleasure sleeves. Pleasure**

Sleeve 1 is also known as 'my mouth,' and Pleasure Sleeve 2 is also known as 'my pussy.' Like the human I'm modeled after, lubrication must be manually inserted into my third pleasure sleeve: my ass."

I stop and glance up from the card to catch Twyla's expression, but her jaw is clenched, and that faraway look is fully activated. I have nothing in her face to go off of, but if it's been written here, I take that as her putting that option on the table.

We've done anal play in the past, but only with my mouth, fingers, and small plugs and toys. There was one attempt with my cock, but my tip barely breached that tightest part of her before the look of misery on her face had me pulling back and never trying again—and that was after an hour of foreplay and preparation that had her literally begging to be filled.

Was that one of the experiences she was referring to, in which she wished I had kept going, pushed her past what I deemed her limit, instead of coming to a full-stop like I did? She hadn't called Red or even Yellow, but I was well acquainted with her body's tendency to freeze when stressed by that point, when she would've been unable to use her safe word even if she wanted to.

But this... this is shedding even more light on what she'd written in the card. And my stomach feels like I've just dropped while riding the world's tallest rollercoaster—exhilarated and full of anticipation for what might come next.

I clear my throat and continue reading. "**Another internal feature that will be tested is the voice-activated speed, depth, and motion controls. Simply touch any part of my body while speaking whatever you'd like me to do. This smart feature uses AI technology that will allow me to learn what your specific commands mean if certain vocabulary isn't initially**

recognized. Plus, I'll eventually anticipate what you'll find pleasurable from patterns in those commands."

I grin and glance up at my doll's now relaxed face as she stares over my shoulder. "So you've got your own built-in algorithm, huh? That's pretty fucking high-tech for just a little fuck toy," I say, being purposely crude to see if I'll get any reaction.

I do, and the one I receive is just as surprising as being offered her asshole on a silver platter.

As perfectly still as my girl is trying her best to remain, she can't control the instinctive slight rock of her hips. Surprising, because it was in direct response to degradation.

Something I've never even dreamed of doing to the woman on my lap. I've never once had the heart to do anything but encourage and praise her, believing any sort of humiliation would traumatize this angelic and sweet-natured creature perched atop my thighs. And before, maybe it would have. But there's no rule that states you can't grow out of a role you once believed you'd be in forever.

Hell, look at me. I thought I'd be a sadistic fuck for the rest of my life, only to give up every ounce of pleasure I derived from pain the moment I met her. And now, I'm evolving once again to be the Dom my sub needs.

So there's nothing to say she can't suddenly discover being degraded arouses her. But I know this woman to the depths of my soul, and I know damn well that while she might find enjoyment from being torn down a bit, it's with anticipation of the building-back-up that might come after. While some subs are masochists who have no want or need for praise after being humiliated, mine is not one of them.

I test my hypothesis.

Leaning forward to speak softly right at her ear, I ask,

"What's a dirty little slut toy need all those smarts for, hmmm?" I hear her swallow thickly. "Shouldn't take much of a brain just to open up and suck my cock like a good little whore, right?"

I can feel her start to tremble where the backs of her thighs press along the tops of mine. Slipping the card behind my back in the seat, both hands now free, I wrap one arm around her hips and reach between her legs with the other. With skilled fingers, I move the gusset of her lace thong aside and trace along her slit, finding exactly what I expected.

"Didn't even have to put you in Test Mode, doll. You're already soaked for me like the perfect little companion I know you are." I thrust one finger up inside her, and she does a damn good job trying to control her breathing, even though the praise makes more slickness seep over my knuckles.

Hypothesis: Confirmed.

Pulling my finger from her hot depths, I use another to move her panties back in place, then lift my hand up between us. I start to open my mouth to suck off her sweetness like I always do, but I try something new instead.

My eyes follow my fingertip as I trace her slightly parted lips, her wetness making it easy as I drag it past the corner, smearing that red lipstick I've been dying to make imperfect since I spotted it on her pretty mouth.

With my hand now cupping her jaw, I order, "All right, dolly. Lick your lips."

When her eyes languidly close and open once more, I refuse the groan that wants to escape me as I watch her sweet little tongue poke out the unsmeared corner of her mouth before making a slow circle around her plump lips, disappearing once she reaches the place it first emerged. And since her eyes never veered from their blank stare past me, the entire act feels surreal, like I've been transported to one of the fictional universes portrayed in *A.I. Artificial Intelligence, The Stepford Wives, Blade Runner, Westworld,* or an episode of *Black Mirror,* and she really is a sex doll come to life.

"Good. Fucking. Girl," I purr against her ear, letting go of her face to grab the card behind me and lean back in the seat to finish reading it. I force myself to concentrate on the words instead of observing her to pick out telltale reactions to the praise I already know she loves.

"Yaddah, yaddah… patterns in those commands—ah. Here we are. **In order to activate Test Mode Two, press the blue button on my remote control. I'll then be able to respond to questions when you place your hand on me, but only with the following phrases: 'Yes, Master.' 'No, Master.' 'Green, Master.' 'Yellow, Master.' And 'Red, Master.' Once Test Mode Two has been initiated, if my auto-lubrication system has not released enough lube into Pleasure Sleeve 2, aka 'my pussy,' it is up to the user to fix the issue. Manual stimulation will be required in order for the desired amount of wetness to express from the refillable internal storage tank before usage. Using any of my three pleasure sleeves without adequate lubrication will likely result in damage to the sleeve. Remember, no refunds. Replacements may be purchased by calling the number on my box.**"

My hand holding the card drops to my lap between us as my head falls back to the leather behind me, my body shaking with silent laughter. Eventually, I lift the other to try to forcefully wipe my grin off my face as I let out a howling sigh, sitting up once again to reach for the remote on the tray table.

"Blue button. Here goes nothin'," I quip, and I press the one beneath the pink one that brought me more delight than I ever could've expected in a single night, and it had only been a warm-up.

A red spotlight turns on from somewhere in the rafters above us, shining a sexy hue across the padded play table to my left. My doll's hands lift to my shoulders, using me to balance as she maneuvers off my lap to stand between my thighs in nothing but her thong, thigh-high socks, and heels.

Another song fills the playroom, and it makes me wonder if she's chosen it as a test of her own. Because surely she picked "WAP" by Cardi B featuring Megan Thee Stallion, a title that literally stands for "wet-ass pussy"—and played it while I'm supposed to check to make sure she's got a wet-ass pussy—to make me laugh, which I definitely am. And combined with all the clever index cards, it's like she did all of it on purpose to see if she could get the darker side of her *Dom* she requested and the lighthearted nature of her *husband* to coexist, not just in the same body but at the same time.

Maybe that's exactly what she wants from me. The degradation *and* the praise. The dark and filthy *and* the playful. The hot and cold side by side instead of one or the other.

The idea is exciting, something I've never consciously considered. It's always been my deviant side *or* my goofy and loving side, never both at once. I probably would've thought it impossible, or at least super challenging. But tonight is proof enough it's not hard at all. And I'm enjoying it thoroughly.

Instead of dancing for me, my little sub points to the lace at her hips, then down at the floor. Still smiling, I blink at the movement, then glance up at her beautiful face.

Her eyes are focused on the wall across the room behind me. When she repeats the movement—tap-tap on each hip with pink-painted pointer fingers, then those same fingers aiming at the ground in perfect sync with the music—I smirk, knowing exactly what I'm supposed to do if following her plan. Yet that darker part of me she purposely woke from hibernation refuses.

But not for long.

I enjoy watching her play out her role with robotic movements one last time before dutifully taking hold of her lacy thong. Just… instead of pulling them down her creamy legs, I fist them tight and suddenly snatch them from her body. Anticipating her jerk toward me, I grip her hips in both my big palms before she even moves an inch, the placement of my hands soothing the sting where the material tore free.

I lick my lips as I drag my eyes up from her bared pussy to her face, catching the sight of her bottom lip just as it pops free of her teeth.

Again, she shows incredible control of herself as she takes two steps back, out of my grasp and from between my legs, turns while keeping her head aligned with her body, then takes the three steps over to the padded table. The curves of her silhouette look extra sensual beneath the red bulb, and my nostrils flare as I watch her climb on top of the play table, then spin to lie down on her back. It's not until her knees bend and rise at the exact same rate and the bottom of her shoes are flat on the table that I stand and saunter over to her.

I start at the side of the table, her body perpendicular like a buffet spread before me, and she keeps her eyes aimed at the ceiling even as I place my palm on her breast and squeeze. I lift a brow and start to move, dragging my hand down her stomach, letting it climb up the stretch of skin exposed of her thigh before reaching the elastic of her sock and across her bent knee, then down her shin as I make my way to the end of the table.

But as amazing as she's been, portraying this character she

was apparently born to play, I see *my* doll peeking through in this position, as her knees are clamped together, even as her feet are pressed into the table as wide as it allows.

And I don't let her get away with it.

Now knowing she can tolerate and even enjoy a little degradation, I call her on her mistake. "What is this?" I ask with mock offense. "What kind of sex doll tries to hide the goods?" I take hold of her knees, gripping one in each hand, then jerk them apart. "Seems this birthday present forgot what she was made for." Sliding my palms ever so slowly down the inside of her thighs, I tell her darkly, "The *only* thing she's good for."

As her muscles tense beneath my hands, I glance up at her face to make sure there's nothing to indicate my words went too far, finding only arousal behind her now half-mast lids, so I continue.

"Come on, little doll. Open these silky thighs and show the user there's no issue to fix," I urge, and her muscles relax, allowing her legs to spread a little farther. "There you go. I'm sure my doll's cunt is already dripping wet, ready to be done with these tests so she can show me what she can really do. Isn't that right, my pretty little fuck toy?"

My eyes are on her pussy as I ask my crude question, my cock throbbing from speaking words I never imagined using during a scene with the sweet creature laid before me, who now resembles a pinned butterfly with pink wings. And I feel a surge of pre-cum release when I see her slit clench before releasing her own delectable juices, forcing a growl past my lips.

Wrapping my arms around her bent legs, I effortlessly yank her to the end of the padded table, a memory flashing through my mind and clouding my vision with the first time I ever tasted her. This exact position, but instead of in a playroom, we were at Doc's beach house, and I feasted on her atop his kitchen counter.

I blink, and a very different version of the same incredible woman fills my eyes. She's no longer that trembling virgin who'd never been pleasured by another person, shyly exposing her tiny body to a man for the first time. No. Before me lays a sensual woman, a body soft with curves I put there when I filled her with my baby. There's nothing shy about her as her arms are stretched above her head, dead weight against the padded surface. Her naked tits proudly pointing at the rafters as the red-tinted light makes their tips a dark-maroon. The nerd version of black fuck-me heels and her pink thigh-high socks making a frame for the porn-worthy image of her pussy that's now glistening with the amount of wetness that's seeped from her slit.

In fact, it's so perfect a vision I'd regret not capturing it, to look at it whenever I want.

Following her index-card instructions, I place my hand against the soft skin of her stomach and order, "Don't move, little doll," then walk over to the tray table to retrieve my cell. When I return, she's exactly how I left her. "Voice commands seem to be working so far," I tease, and I aim the camera, aligning it horizontally to show from the tip of one knee, across her center, to the other.

The flash goes off, and she startles, her legs closing the slightest bit before my growl stops her.

"Don't. Fucking. Move."

And although my hand isn't on her, she follows my command.

I take another picture from the same angle, this time with the flash off so it'll capture the red light and what it does to the image of her body. Satisfied with the result of both photos, I move my phone, switching between flash and no flash, as I take more pictures from all different angles, mesmerized as I see the tiny reactions my doll's body is having to the impromptu photo shoot.

She might feel embarrassed or awkward, but she's getting off on the discomfort.

Masochistic.

Because it doesn't have to be *physical* pain that sexually arouses someone in order for them to be considered a masochist.

A part of me wants to deep-dive into the reasoning behind why these feelings have awoken inside her. And I will, along with scheduling a visit with Doc at his earliest convenience. But for now, for tonight's scene, I'll just be extra careful as we dip our toes in, allowing her to experience a kiddie-pool version of a masochist getting to play with a former professional sadist... before tossing her into the deep end.

I walk to the head of the padded table and set my phone there, keeping it handy in case other positions I put her in speak to me and demand I capture them.

Trailing a finger from the center of her palm and along one of her outstretched arms still above her head as I stroll toward my spot at the other end, I glimpse her open eyes as she stares up at the rafters. I take a moment to check in with her, because she appears to be dissociating.

"Color, doll?"

Without missing a beat, she responds, "Green, Master," punctuating it with one of her practiced blinks.

"Very good girl," I purr, then continue back down her body until I'm positioned at the foot of the table, staring at the most intensely cock-hardening image I've ever viewed in my life. "If you were real, I'd make you look at yourself right now, so you could see how maddeningly sexy you are, little doll. But, alas, you're not. You're a mindless object meant to be used for my pleasure. And according to your instructions, we need to complete this step before I get to do that. So let's proceed, shall we?"

It's a test, and I'm really starting to like this game.

She doesn't answer—because as a doll, she hasn't been "programmed" to unless my hand is on her—passing with flying colors.

And little things are starting to occur to me about this whole situation she's orchestrated.

As a doll, she doesn't have to speak more than a simple yes, no, or color. She doesn't have to try to answer naughty questions I might pose, which a lot of the time makes her choke up and freeze. This scene takes all that off her plate.

"I guess… since you're just a toy, I don't need to bother with gentle caresses and sweet kisses to make you pliable and needy. So in that case…."

That's all the notice my sub gets before I slide two fingers deep into her pussy. I smile to myself when her head arches back and her lips part as she gasps, her eyes flaring with life. I see her throat work as she swallows, forcing herself back into character, and fighting to stay there as I start to move my fingers.

Swirling them inside her, I say as if speaking to myself, "Ooh, impressive. Yeah, that's nice and tight. Hot too. Funny, I don't remember reading anything about a heating feature." I curl my fingers to press upward, dragging them over that extra-soft spot that makes her shudder. "And look at that! The lubrication system really does release more when you stimulate this particular little cock sleeve." I thrust them deep, watching her face for any hint of a wince as I test her sweet cunt the way I would examine a pocket pussy—roughly. But there's nothing but pleasure there, even as I can tell she's trying to keep her expression neutral.

Without warning, I pull my hand away, and the shock of going from being finger-fucked to completely empty without any gradual deceleration makes her whimper.

"Huh?" I stride to the head of the table, twisting my face with mock confusion and making a show of leaning over my doll's face and peering down at her. "I could've sworn my toy made a sound." She doesn't meet my eyes as she clenches her teeth together, and I choose to ignore her panting, since she does such a damn good job of keeping her expression blank while she tries to catch her breath. It's not until she blinks those long lashes slow and steady that I put her out of her misery. "I must've been hearing things." And then I lift my sticky fingers to my nose, staring down at her as I inhale deeply.

My eyes close when my lungs near capacity, and I groan through my exhale, opening them once again as I place the two digits coated in her cream into my mouth and suck them clean. "Mmm… this lube is fucking delicious." I lean over her and lick my lips. "I should leave them a five-star review for the flavor alone."

And as if my cock wasn't already fighting to break free from its confines…

My doll blushes before my eyes.

Face neutral. A faraway look past my right ear. Smeared red lips slightly parted. She's utterly still as she flushes, a shade of crimson I can see clearly because the red light turned off as the song ended while I was busy thrusting my fingers hard and deep inside her wet-ass pussy.

Cupping her heated cheek in the palm of my hand, I ask,

"Little doll, will one of the buttons make you take off my clothes?" and something flickers in her eyes before she replies.

"Yes, Master."

"Which one? Because if I don't get my pants off soon, I'm going to lose circulation in my cock."

She doesn't respond, and a grin spreads across my face.

"God, you're fucking good at this, doll," I praise, and then I step away from her, because now I know it's part of her plan to strip me herself.

And I need to stop fucking with her so we can make that happen.

CHAPTER 17

Seven

SHE SITS up from the table, turning robotically to the side until her legs are dangling before she hops off. Even in her high chunky heels and with me completely barefoot, she doesn't quite reach my chin. She spins, peels a card from beneath the table, and lifts it between us.

I take it immediately.

"If Test Mode 2 met your satisfaction, I'm ready to be played with. The next four buttons on my remote are as follows:

Purple—Blowjob (Auto Mode). Description: I have been programmed to perform fellatio on my user. Sit back, relax, and enjoy the preset blowjob, or use my voice-activated controls to change the speed, depth, and motion. Blowjob (Auto Mode) is for a mostly hands-free experience in which I can do all the work for you. My AI will be active during this mode to update the preset with your preferences. The more you use the voice controls, the better my blowjob will become.

Yellow—Blowjob (Manual Mode). Description: I have been programmed to shut down all presets and functions except for my lubrication system and vocal responses, which will remain active as you take control of the blowjob. This is the mode you should use for a hands-on, self-pleasure experience. Use my Pleasure Sleeve 1 as you would any other male masturbation device, colloquially known as fleshlights or strokers, by moving yourself in and out of it however you like. As your own personal Intimacy Companion, I'm here to take it."

I'm forced to break away from reading the instructions aloud, as I groan at the filthy line my innocent doll wrote. Never has my girl said anything so direct and challenge-inducing. There's nothing else she could have said that would spark my experimental nature more. It instantaneously makes me want to see just how far she's willing for me to "take" her.

I take a moment to think about the woman behind the controller's buttons. I'm in absolute awe of how perfect this situation is for both of us, how thoroughly thought out this scene is that she created. I don't think I could've come up with a better scenario myself. Hell, I don't think I could've come up with anything nearly this good, when it comes to a scene that would help her get past her unwanted limits and guide her to a new level of submission.

The blowjob's automatic mode? How I can "voice control" her? Absolutely brilliant for giving her Dom what he wants by following his detailed instructions, taking the guesswork out of it so she doesn't have to worry that she's not doing something right.

And the manual mode, telling me to use her mouth however I see fit… Jesus Christ. Challenge accepted.

"If at any time during Blowjob (Manual Mode) my sensors

detect possible impending damage to Pleasure Sleeve 1, some of my other functions will come back online, and I will tap your leg three times to let you know you should stop immediately. Again, my vocal response system will remain active during manual mode, so feel free to ask yes/no questions and check color."

My smart girl. Tapping my leg three times—a safety precaution we've always had for our scenes. A nonverbal safeword, in case she's unable to speak… like if she's gagged or her mouth is full of my cock.

"My orange and green buttons are much the same as purple and yellow, but they activate Pleasure Sleeve 2 and have additional functions.

Orange—Auto Fuck. Programmed with a preset. I will follow voice commands and continually learn what my user enjoys for future play. If I do not follow a vocalized instruction, it is because I am unfamiliar with the vocabulary you chose to speak. Simply place your hand on me as you did during Test Mode 2, say the command again, and then make me do what that command means. It will save this new vocabulary and the movements you create with my body together in my system for all future use. Use this button (Orange) for a more interactive experience between the two of us.

Green—Manual Fuck. All systems besides lubrication and vocal responses shut down. I do not learn or save anything for future playtime. This mode requires you to position me the way you want me at all times while activated. Generally speaking, I become a mindless toy for you to enjoy much like the Sex Doll models that came before me. Like Pleasure Sleeve 1 in Manual Mode, use Pleasure Sleeve 2 like you would a male masturbator, and if at any time Manual Fuck is in use

and my sensors detect possible impending damage to Pleasure Sleeve 2, some of my other functions will come back online, and I will say "Red, Master" or tap your leg three times to let you know you should stop immediately."

If I weren't beginning to feel like a drug addict desperately in need of their next fix, I'd take the time to revel in everything my doll is offering. But the moment I read "I become a mindless toy," I damn near came in my too-tight pants. It's time I play with my new present.

"Feel free to switch between these four buttons whenever you like. Finally, as mentioned in the first instruction, the final button (Red) is the emergency stop. If at any time you need to completely shut down your new Intimacy Companion, press this button. Thank you, and enjoy."

Dropping the card to the floor, since I memorized what each button signifies the moment I read it, I waste no more time. As badly as I want to jump right in and go for my favorite color—green—I know my doll put the buttons in the order she'd like me to follow for her scene, so I press Purple.

As soon as the music starts—a techno song I recognize and know we have set in our Playtime Playlist to continuously repeat until it's manually changed—my doll turns robotically, then I watch her sexy naked ass as she walks back over to the new leather chair. Without looking in my direction, keeping that neutral face she's damn near perfected tonight, she gets into position on her knees, then sinks back to rest her ass on those heels. When her hands come to rest palms up on the tops of her thighs, that's all it takes to send me into action.

I lift my right leg high enough to step over her flawless Nadu —the name of the submissive or *Gorean slave* pose she's in—so that I'm now standing straddling her knees, which are parted exactly the way I like and taught her all those years ago. Before I can sit down though, her hands rise, her eyes level with my thighs and not lifting as she takes hold of my pants and boxer briefs and pulls them down at once. I sink before her until my ass meets the leather seat, and I lift my bare feet enough for her to pull everything off the rest of the way.

Whether or not she had plans to take off my shirt, I'm too hot to wait any longer, and I strip my Henley over my head, tossing it on top of the perfectly folded bundle she created with my other clothes. Even playing this new character role, she's still following the rules as my submissive. Well… all except the very easy one she forgot before this party got started, when she left all her stuff strewn about instead of placing them in the trunk. But there's nothing that could make me punish her for that little slip, now knowing what was on her mind and the anxiety she must've been feeling when she was getting ready to give me this unimaginable gift. A minor detail like storing her items would've been the very last thing on her mind.

Now, though, recognizing she's relaxed enough to remember her rituals, I reach out to stroke her soft cheek. "That's my good little doll. Thank you for taking care of my things like you've been trained."

Normally, she'd reply with *"you're welcome, Master,"* but since it's not part of her few "programmed vocal responses," I allow it when she tells me, "Yes, Master," instead.

Additionally, she's not to come out of Nadu—the position she's to start every scene in—until she's given a very specific command, which I give her this time while still stroking the smooth skin of her beautiful face.

"And we begin."

She launches forward, as if she's been anticipating those

three words for weeks. And maybe she has. Weeks of planning, training, practicing, and anxiously preparing to give me a birthday I'd never forget. The force of her impact, her palms flat against my overheated skin, one in the middle of my chest, the other centered on my abs, shoves my back against the seat, the air leaving my lungs. Not from the having the wind knocked out of me, but because as I was moving backward, she kept moving toward me, her mouth aligned with my cock.

That first moment, the sensation of my sensitive tip slipping right past those plump, smeared red lips and into her hot, wet mouth, was so exquisite it took my breath away.

I groan, watching her perform for me once again. Eyes now closed, she uses the techniques I taught her, the tender ones I love because she's the one using them. Swirls of her tongue around the fat head. Running her closed wet lips or her tongue up and down my shaft like a popsicle.

Her blowjobs are teasing and sensual, slow and erotic. Always used as a form of foreplay and never the main event, because I'd need a lot more stimulation to actually reach orgasm than what I've ever been willing to take from her sweet mouth.

As she brings one hand down from where her palms always seemingly unconsciously stroke my hairy chest and stomach while she pleasures me with her mouth, she then grips the bottom of my rod before taking my tip back inside to suck me. Her second hand joins the first, and with her fists around my erection stacked on top of each other, my mushroom head and the few inches below it are all she needs to focus on with her mouth. Just enough to feel really fucking arousing for me without worrying I'll go too deep and hurt her.

I taught her the stacked hands trick more as a way to block too much of my cock from slipping through her lips, for my peace of mind, than as a way to have the rest of my shaft included in the blowjob.

But now, after everything she said in the card, and after reading her instructions specifically pertaining to blowjobs, I know I've gone too easy on her and for too long. So long that my doll feels the need to spice things up in our sex life—which I cannot believe is something anyone would ever have to do when it comes to *me*.

My, how the mighty have fallen.

But not for long.

Sliding my fingers through her hair behind her ear, then around to the back of her head, I see her eyes open in surprise before they close again, feeling her movements falter for a moment before she continues her sweet teasing. But now that my hand is right where I want it, a place of power and control, I want more from my little sub. Knowing she wants to learn to give me more, I feel a carnal desire to teach her, then take it all.

"Let's see how well this AI system works," I tell her, and her nostrils flare as she steals a breath while she continues to suck on those top few inches. "Remove your right hand."

As soon as the order leaves my lips, her top fist falls to the top of my thigh, but she keeps working that hot mouth of hers on the tip of my dick.

"Mmm, very good. Now that freed up several more inches of cock for my new doll to break in her pleasure sleeve with." When she doesn't attempt to put more of my shaft in her mouth, I tighten my grip at the back of her head, and she gasps. Just as her mouth opens around my girth, I pull her toward me, sliding deeper along her hot tongue. When her lips close again, she moans, and the pleasured sound is music to my soul as it vibrates down my dick and into my balls, making me match her with a groan of my own.

"There you go, little toy. Save that vocabulary for later. But I guess I need to be more specific in my commands than just mere suggestions. So now, I want you to drool. Release more with that lubrication system of yours, because I want to see you spit on my cock. And after you do that, I want you to jack me with that tight little fist," I tell her.

But she doesn't stop what she's doing, continuing to just hold my erection steady while she sucks on the extra couple of inches I forced into her mouth.

I can tell—not only by her not following the command as quickly as she had when I told her to drop one hand, but because of the way her breaths through her nose are coming faster and faster—that she's reaching one of her limits I now know she wants me to help her break. Even though she's not *frozen* in fear, she's stuck in a loop she's unable to come out of, and it's my job to save her. Only this time, I won't be stopping the scene to pull her into my arms and tell her everything is okay.

My hand in her hair, I gently but forcefully tug her off my cock, and demand an answer, "Color?"

"Green, Master," she pants out, surprising me, and I feel a surge of precum rise to my tip.

I had expected either "yellow" or, most likely, silence—her usual response when she's under the spell of her fear instincts—so hearing her all-clear response after absolutely no hesitation is a fucking delightful shock to my system, feeding even more life back into my domination.

Plus, the life in her face instead of the blank look she's held all night, even with her eyes still closed, brings me comfort I didn't realize I was missing. Now recognizing I need the animation in her expression to safely continue tonight's scene, I pull her close and lean down to whisper in her ear.

"I'm so damn proud of how well you've played your role tonight, little doll. And I don't want you to stop. Everything you've prepared for tonight has been perfect beyond my imagination, and I love you so goddamn much for these gifts you're giving me." I feel her shudder, knowing she always loves the feel of my breath as I speak softly, just for her to hear, right next to her skin. Especially when it's words of praise I'm feeding directly into her brilliant mind. "But in order for me to give you what we both want, I need my new toy to update her system to include lifelike facial expressions so incredible I won't be able to tell you're not real. Otherwise, it won't be safe to continue, because I won't be able to *'read your mind,'* as you believe I do. Understand?"

"Yes, Master," she replies breathily, and I pull her back enough I can see them when she blinks her eyes open. Not in the slow, eerie way she's been doing ever since we started playing, but in a very human way that clears her vision and meets my loving gaze.

"There you are." I smile down at her, her hair still gripped in my fist, not in a painful hold but one of stability and control. Her lips tilt up in the corners to give me a hint of a smile of her own. But I can see she's still fearful of the order I gave her that she hasn't followed yet, because she knows now I won't be letting her off the hook like I always have before. "Now. Be my good little fuck doll, and spit on my cock."

The red flush that steals up from her naked tits all the way to her pigtails sets off every sadistic pleasure receptor that has laid dormant within me since the day I met this woman.

When she doesn't make a move yet again, I raise an eyebrow, using a tone with her she's never heard before.

"Spit on my cock, or I'll make you gag on it."

She gasps, blinking rapidly, but when she feels my grip tighten slightly at the back of her head and she can't get away, it's like she's finally able to snap out of freeze and into fight mode. But instead of fighting *me,* the person inducing the fear response, she fights herself and whatever it is within her that makes her believe she can't do something, even when she wants so badly to follow my commands.

I watch her jaw move, my heart rate rising and my breaths deepening, as she works to gather her saliva. And then, pulling her eyes away from mine to look down as much as my grip allows, she aims the best she can and forces herself to let the pitiful amount of spit she collected drip from her pretty mouth.

No matter the amount though, my cock jerks, as if reaching out to catch it like an offering, and I feel the warm wetness hit the side of my shaft. I look down just as it drips off, then look back up at my sub.

"Good. Fucking. Girl," I growl, just before I yank her to me and kiss her so hard it momentarily hurts. But the pain feels good and eggs me on, and I force her lips open with my tongue, diving inside. "You did it."

I feel her smile at the praise, and the power I feel being able to make her feel good about herself is intoxicating as fuck.

"You're going to do it again, little doll," I tell her against her mouth as I continue to ravage it with my own. "But this time, I'm going to help you get it *juuust* right. And then you're going to carry out the rest of my command, wrap that little hand around your master's big cock, and jack me off. Got it?" I punctuate the question with a tiny jerk of my hand controlling her head, and the aggression in my tone and slight movement is enough to keep her instincts at bay.

"Yes, Master," she whimpers when I let her lips free enough that she can respond, and I feel even more of my old self unfurl.

And God, it feels so good.

She lets out a shocked little sound that makes more precum seep from my tip when I start feeding my own saliva into her mouth as we kiss.

"Don't swallow," I hint, and after a moment, she gives me a barely perceptible nod of understanding.

This kiss is fucking hot and messy. It's goddamn arousing, and not just for me, as I feel my doll's hands come up to grip my legs, tiny tugs, as if trying to pull my much larger body toward her, that seem unconscious. Her kneeling body between my legs moves, her hips making small, sensual circles, similar to her movements when she was on my lap, dancing for me earlier. As if she wishes she had a cock to sit on while I shove more of my spit into her mouth with my tongue.

When I feel it's enough that it's now a continuous dribble out the corners of our lips, I pull away suddenly with a growl and drag her face-first toward my awaiting erection that's so hard it's damn near painful.

"Now, *spit,*" I demand, and this time, there's no hesitation, and it's no tiny little wad of white bubbles that leave my submissive's lips. My doll gathers all of our combined saliva that pooled beneath her tongue during our kiss, and with her mouth so close there's no way she can miss, I lean back and tilt my head for the perfect view as she follows her master's orders.

"*Fuck* yeah. That's my perfect little slut doll," I growl as she pumps my cock using our spit as lubrication. Her responding whimper along with her other hand slipping between her thighs lets me know the combination of praise and degradation is more than welcome. It's desired. So hungry for it that she not only breaks character but one of my rules.

Immediately, I grab the remote and hit the yellow button. The change in song is enough to snap her to attention, and I see the moment she realizes what she's doing. Startled, like the fingers massaging her pussy lips aren't her own, she snatches her hand away, making a fist and pressing it to the top of her thigh. She drops the other from my cock, remembering that all her systems as a mindless toy have been shut down with the press of a button.

As much as I want to watch her jack my cock with one hand while playing with herself with the other, I couldn't allow the indiscretion to go on. What kind of Dom would I be if I let my submissive get away with disobedience?

CHAPTER 18
Twyla

OH, *shit*.

CHAPTER 19

Seven

THE INNOCENT AND slightly confused surprise still in her pretty eyes would've been my undoing just hours ago, making me want to cuddle her and tell her she did nothing wrong. But instead, those emotions I see in her expression bring me sadistic pleasure, especially knowing that deep inside, she wants my corrections and punishments. Because it'll teach her what she craves to learn.

"Something's wrong with my new toy." I sigh and lean forward, resting my forearms on my wide-spread knees and clasping my hands between us. She's back in Nadu, but following her rituals now won't make up for breaking my rules. "For some reason, it started touching its second pleasure sleeve by itself. And I definitely didn't use voice commands to make it do that."

Another test—to see if she responds in any way to being called "it" for the first time.

She swallows thickly, but it's hard to tell whether she's

reacting to the objectification or that I pointed out her indiscretion. Either way, she doesn't flinch away, so I'll leave it as an option unless she says or shows me in some capacity that she doesn't like it.

"We can't have you taking liberties outside your generic preset without my orders now, can we?" I ask, rhetorical, but she still knows she's required to verbally acknowledge what I say.

"No, Master," she whispers, glancing up from my laced fingers to quickly steal a look at my expression.

She's the only sub I've ever allowed to see my face, to look into my eyes, as I dominate her. It's a hard limit of hers, one I'd never discourage. She needs the ability to see the love in my gaze, so she doesn't ever have to worry that I'm actually disappointed in her. Plus, eye contact for someone as shy as her is hard as fuck to begin with, so if she can will herself to do that, then I wouldn't admonish her in the first place.

"No… no, we can't," I add through a sigh. "So, I guess my only option, if I want to continue enjoying my doll's mouth, is to take over controlling it."

I stand abruptly, the movement making the leather chair skid back a few inches, eliciting a godawful sound that makes her jolt even more than suddenly having my cock looming over her from above.

I reach down and stroke my fingers through her hair, petting her a moment, and her head tilts into the tender touch. "Your jumpiness has always been so delightful to the part of me that feeds on fear." I take hold of her chin and lift her face to look at me, which has to be an incredibly imposing view from her position. "While you've been so worried your undying innocence and easy embarrassment is annoying and undesirable, little did you know it's what's kept the kenneled sadist inside me alive all this time. Like a continuous supply of the finest filets thrown into its cage, keeping it strong but tethered, not shitty scraps here and there that barely keep it conscious."

She trembles, her eyes shuttering, and I sense relief mixed with her anxiety over what I might do to her. Still holding her chin, I stroke her cheek with my thumb where her lipstick is smeared even more since being in her mouth, and I glance at my cock, smirking when I see it's stained as well. I like her marks on me.

My grip on her chin tightens, and with my thumb near the side of her mouth, when I squeeze, her plump lips purse. Her brow furrows at the unfamiliar hold, and when I squeeze even tighter, her eyes pop open in confusion. The feel of this grip on anyone's face is at the very least slightly humiliating, knowing how silly the person clutching your cheeks is making you look, on top of the inability to move away.

I squeeze harder, and where my fingers press, she has no choice but to open her mouth, and she lets out a delicious whimper.

"Three taps on my leg, little doll," I remind her, and her eyes flare.

"Yesh, Mashtah," her response comes out garbled, and the flush that covers her face when she hears herself is like gasoline on the flame that's been lit inside me.

My big hand on her petite features looks almost cruel, but I'm careful that the only thing she feels is uncomfortable as I open her mouth wider, pulling her forward by her jaw until the tip of my cock is right at her skewed lips. Wrapping my other hand around my manscaped base, I tap her face with the underside of my dick, right across her mouth, but I'm long and girthy, so it covers a lot more area. She blinks rapidly, unfamiliar with this flavor of degradation, but she makes no attempt to pull away. I'd feel even the tiniest jerk if she tried to move back, but instead, she sinks into my hold. Either she's liking it or she's just giving in to her sex-doll role, but either way, there have been no taps on my leg.

I slap my cock on the cushion of her smooshed lips again, smirking when precum blesses her face. She gasps when she feels it, and I let go of my shaft to swipe it up with my finger, then press it into her mouth and smear it on her tongue.

"Did you know, little doll, that the tool a priest uses to sprinkle and sling holy water is called an *aspergillum*?" I grip my cock tightly and point it straight out from my body, sliding my knuckles up to force more precum out the tip.

"No, Mashtah," she replies, her voice trembling slightly as she watches the clear bead emerge. I lift my rod just in time so that it doesn't drip off quite yet.

"There are a couple of different kinds, but the most common nowadays is a handle attached to a hollow metal ball with small holes at the tip. The priest dips it into the bucket of holy water, known as the *aspersorium*, and after the ball fills up, he lifts it into the air—" I take hold of the base of my shaft again. "—then whips it over the congregation." I slap her pillowy lips once more, and just like before, the sticky proof of how fucking hot I am for this woman kneeling at my feet splats, this time across her forehead.

Her face is the reddest I've ever seen it, and not letting go of her face, I squat and reach between her spread thighs without warning.

Just as I suspected, I find my sub completely drenched.

So much for humiliation being a punishment. I'll have to think of something later.

She's so wet I don't even have to dip my finger inside her slit to feel it. Her pussy lips are coated so thoroughly it makes me salivate, and I have to fight the urge to force her onto her back, cover her entire cunt with my mouth, and suck her clean. Instead, I pacify myself by swirling my middle three fingertips together from her clit, through her folds, and back again, then lifting them to suck off her cream.

She whines and wiggles in my clutch, and I stand back up to my full height.

"Looks like I blessed you and made you all wet, my little worshipper." I smear my precum that's on her forehead horizontally with my thumb, smirking once again when I then drag it vertically through the middle. "The power of your *user* compels you, *doll*." And then, dick in hand, I press my crown to the cunt I've made of her lips, finally releasing them as I start to press inside.

I continue to grip her jaw but move my other hand to hold the back of her head. "Mmm… tight little cock sleeve. Hope it's ready to be broken in."

She moans around my girth, her eyes fluttering closed as I feed her just the usual amount. She relaxes more and more as I pull her head backward, then tug her forward over and over, making her take nothing extra than I always have. There's no resistance in her muscles as I move her back and forth instead of holding her still and thrusting my hips forward and back, using her mouth just like I would a stroker.

"That's right. You're my mindless little fuck toy. I'm just using a storebought hole to bounce on my cock for my own solo pleasure," I say for her benefit, letting her know she's doing exactly what she's supposed to—absolutely nothing.

And she's fucking loving it. When I take in her beautiful face, every feature is completely at ease. There's no furrowing of her brow in concentration to try to blow me just right. There's no shifting of her eyes behind her closed lids while searching her mind for tips and tricks. Even her lips have gone slack around my cock, her jaw malleable instead of stiff in my grip to create suction or guard her teeth. Her breaths went from anxious shallow panting to now steady and deep, and somehow my dick hardens even further.

It occurs to me I left my phone on the playtable, and I instantly regret that I can't snap a photo or record a few seconds of this moment.

It almost makes me feel guilty to bring her out of this peace she's found, this newly discovered way to shut down her mind and float along a level of consciousness that's nearly impossible for people like her to reach. People with brains that constantly run at full-power and don't understand the meaning of "relax." I know because I was just like her—and still am, outside the playroom—until I discovered Domination, using it to control not only other people but my own mind as well. Hyperfocusing on a submissive and clearing out all the chatter. Domspace, which feels similar to the way subspace has been described to me by so many in the community.

It's blissful.

And like I said, it almost makes me feel guilty to not allow her to stay in this peaceful state. *Almost* being the keyword. But not quite, since I now know how to get her here with ease, and right this minute, my doll is in the middle of an important lesson.

Pushing her away until only the very tip of my cock is still between her lax lips, I focus completely on *her* entire being and not the sensations along my dick as I then pull her mouth back onto me, this time an inch deeper than before.

No reaction.

There's not one reaction on her part, which is a better outcome for what she's asked me to teach her, even though my sadistic side is slightly disappointed she didn't at least show a sign of acknowledgement that she noticed. Nevertheless, she earns some quiet praise as I continue to use her mouth at this new depth.

"That's a good little toy," I murmur down at her, a soothing tone to keep her in this glorious state. "Look how pretty you are with your user's fat cock in your mouth."

She sighs and becomes heavier in my hands, which tells me she's surrendered even more to this scene.

God, the power she's giving me right now. How powerful she makes me *feel.*

Off and on I pull her.

Out and back in I go.

And slowly, I pick up my pace while keeping the depth steady each time I enter her mouth. Sweat starts to slicken my skin as my full concentration zeroes in on controlling the speed and the amount of cock I feed her. I'm vaguely aware my hand has tightened in her hair as my muscles have tensed, but the way she's just taking it without a single wince tells me she probably hasn't even noticed that either.

Then, I see it, and if I weren't the man of control that I've proven I am, I would fill her throat with my cum the moment it happens.

My doll, the one who's innocent to the point of prim and proper when she gives me head, who's always mortified when something I wouldn't think twice about happens, like when a line of spit connects her lips to my cock as I pull out of her mouth…

That doll…

Begins to drool.

At first, it's a single dribble out one corner of her still-relaxed lips, and I watch it trickle down her chin like a raindrop on a windowpane, staring in utter fascination as it then turns into a rivulet of saliva gaining in length. I prepare myself, wondering what will happen when that sexy-as-fuck bomb of wetness lands. From my angle above her, my head cocked to the side so I can keep an eye on my even strokes, I see it's aimed right for the middle of her thigh.

But I refuse to stop. I refuse to end this delectable feeling of power over my sub who's enjoying it just as much as I am as I control her head, moving her off and on my cock until I've lulled her into oblivion.

Yet, she's going to feel it. And I'll need to respond accordingly to her reaction. She's going to feel it splash on her heated skin, realize what she allowed to happen in her complete submission, and freak the fu—

It disconnects from her chin and hits. Not a tiny teardrop that could go unnoticed, but a whole stream of saliva that pools on the top of her leg before finally overflowing, forming a miniature waterfall over the inside of her thigh.

I don't realize I'm holding my breath until her sexy moan snaps me out of it. A sweet little coo around my cock that makes me instinctively thrust my hips when I pull her forward, giving her another couple of inches.

When she takes it with ease, I groan with pride. "Fucking Christ. What a perfect little whore doll you are, taking so much of my cock without complaint."

She coos again, and with so much saliva, it makes a gargling sound, and I brace internally when she instinctively swallows to avoid choking on her spit. But nothing changes in her demeanor, her submission intoxicating, a temptation the sadist within me cannot resist any longer, as I pull her onto my cock until the tip touches the very back of her mouth. It's only for a split second before I push her off again, but—

"My fucking God." No objection. So I do it again just as deep, then tug her backward. "I've never seen anything—" In and out. "—as fucking sexy—" Back and forth. "—as my big cock—" Pull and push. "—disappearing—" In and out. "—inside my fuck doll's—" Back and forth. "—slutty little mouth."

By the time I get all that out, I'm truly masturbating with my sweet submissive's head, not only yanking her back and forth with my powerful grip but thrusting forward on her intake. And her only response is the continuous hum during her exhales that are momentarily shut off each time my cock meets her throat.

"You love being used, don't you, baby?" I growl, keeping a tight rein on my movements as I try to balance the Dom I've always been with her and the Seven I used to be.

Because in the past, if a sub had shown she loved this act as much as my doll is in this moment, it would've been all I needed as the green light to shove myself all the way inside without a second thought. No remorse. But the subs of my past were highly masochistic, ones with awe-inspiring tolerances for pain that even I wouldn't be able to take. And while I cared about their safety, mental and physical, I was never responsible for the emotional part, and I only played with partnered subs who had their own Dominant to handle aftercare.

My doll is the only submissive I've ever loved. She's the only woman I've ever been responsible for taking care of in all aspects of her being and safety.

And that's why instead of giving into more sadistic temptations, I don't push her any further physically. I don't give her more of my length to test just how far I can go before she starts to struggle. This has been a purely positive situation, and there's no point in ruining that just for the sake of trying to find a line in the sand. There will be time to continue that search later.

But I *will* push her a bit further mentally, just because I want to.

With my pace and depth steady, my grip still strong in her hair and on her jaw, I use words to test my sub's new trick.

"This toy takes my dick so easily," I murmur, my voice taking on a slightly bullying tone. "What a little whore you are, dolly, letting this fat cock skull-fuck you without you even flinching." She moans, her lips closing around my shaft as I pump in and out of her. "Look at you, trying to swallow even more of me. If I didn't know better, I'd think my present had already been played with."

Finally, *finally*, I get a reaction. A subtle tightening around her eyes that draws her brows a tiny bit closer together. And now I know where one limit lies within her newfound interest in degradation.

My doll doesn't like the idea of someone else using her this way. Which is good, because I would never allow that to happen. But depending on how much she comes to enjoy playing with her masochistic side, we might be able to purposely use this limit for some psychological-torture fun in the future—that is, if it turns out to be a soft limit and not a hard one, which I'd never fuck around with.

But this is where I choose to stop pushing, testing these

particular boundaries—at least when it comes to this part of the scene, without having been inside her pussy yet.

The past several minutes have been a milestone—hell, a *life event*—for my doll. For our D/s relationship. Something I'll never forget, feeling her completely surrender within my hands, trusting me to fuck her face however I saw fit.

I slide out of her mouth but don't let go of her head, and the look of pure satisfaction on her beautiful face from just submitting to my pleasure brings me to my knees, literally. I drop to my haunches before her, a gasp finally leaving her lips as I pull her forward once again, not onto my cock but to my face, so I can kiss her in a way I've never kissed anyone in my life. I kiss her hard and thorough, messy and primal, lapping at the wetness around her lips and down her chin from my not-so-gentle fucking. I taste not only her mouth's sweetness but the saltiness of what I left behind, and I glance down to watch more of it leak out of my crown.

CHAPTER 20

Seven

I'VE NEVER FELT excitement like this, of being filthier than I've ever been with my innocent doll.

When I met her, I'd already done every kinky thing imaginable, so I never felt like I missed out on anything when I "settled down" and married her. I'd gotten it all out of my system by then, and it felt completely natural to tame my dominance back to a level suited for the only woman I'd ever fallen in love with. Absolutely no regrets. None. Not a single one.

But tonight feels like a whole new existence of its own. It feels like discovering this incredible alternative world all over again. Getting to show my wife a side of me and a higher tier of pleasure that I never even dreamed she'd be open to—it feels like I've gotten close to enlightenment. Like the whole fucking meaning of life has been whispered in my ear.

My arousal grows to a fever pitch, to a point that I don't care about her birthday plans any longer. I need to be inside her. I need to consume her.

She's giving me more than just her complete submission with no more limits of her own.

She's giving me a part of myself back that I truly didn't miss until the moment I got to experience a taste of it with her. Yet it feels like a whole new world, and I only want to share this one with her.

I reach behind me and grab the remote, clicking the green button. "Right now, I have no use for the orange button. You can show me what you had planned for the auto-fuck part of the scene some other time. Because at the moment, seeing how fucking blissed out you are after relinquishing all control to my will, all I want to do is see if I can continue to put that look on your face with my cock in Pleasure Sleeve 2."

She smiles drunkenly, and I stand, pulling her with me, not stopping until I pick her up and she instinctively wraps her legs around my waist. I step over to the playtable once again, setting her naked ass on the very end, and the image of her earlier in the same spot—how beautiful she was, sprawled out and helpless, trusting me to only follow the instructions of the scene she laid out—fills my head.

But now, with the green button pushed, and a new song playing over the speakers, there are no rules. She's giving me free rein to do whatever I want to her with the specific instruction to push her *past* all her limits.

Yet… with the way I feel right now, more aroused than I've ever been in my entire life, if I were to slip my cock into her sopping-wet heat, I would once again turn into that young man receiving his first lap dance. Only I'd be that same young man feeling the most exquisite pussy to ever exist, resulting in me filling her with my cum before I even got my tip fully inside.

Plus, I need to prepare her for the rough fucking she'll soon be taking. A roughness I know for a fact that she's never experienced before, because I'm the only man who's ever had the pleasure of fucking her—gently or otherwise.

With my hand pressed to the center of her chest, I push her down until she's lying flat on the padded table, her thigh-high-covered legs and naughty Mary Janes dangling off the end on either side of me. I step from between them, keeping my palm on her chest as I walk around the table to the opposite end, spotting my phone I'd left here earlier and moving it out of the way. Then, I take hold of her biceps in both my hands, and I pull, sliding her quickly up the playtable until her legs are stretched out and her feet rest atop the other end.

I take both her wrists and tug her arms straight above her head, commanding her to "stay" when I let go and walk over to the wall of leather cuffs and restraints. Choosing the ones I know fit her delicate wrists, I slide them off their hooks and take them back over to her. I make quick work of binding her arms together, then attaching them to the metal loop on the underside of the table with a leather strap.

"Color?" I ask when she doesn't make a move to test her restraints, hoping she isn't already frozen in fear.

"Green, Master," she says dreamily, and I feel my lips pull into a secret smile. Never has my doll sounded so relaxed when she's first been bound. She's always, *always* been apprehensive and required time to settle into the position, ever since that one traumatic night from our past. But tonight has been special in a way we haven't even begun to dissect yet, and I'm sure when we look back, it will be this birthday we attribute to a lot of healing and new beginnings.

I walk over to the wall once again and open a cabinet, finding a bottle of the lube I know works best for my sub's body

—water based and scentless, perfect for her sensitive skin and chemistry. Every Dom should remember details such as this; it's part of the proper care and keeping of a submissive, to ensure they stay healthy and safe.

Sure, they can order their sub to keep such things supplied for their use. But what if their sub accidently grabs the wrong thing, or something gets swapped without their knowledge? It would be just as much the Dom's fault for not knowing it was wrong, or knowing and not double checking it was correct.

Hence another reason why being a Dominant is a huge responsibility and nothing at all like what the fuckboys on dating sites think it is. It's not all spankings and furry handcuffs while telling your one-night stand to call you Daddy. It's a relationship based on more trust than even a solid marriage requires and not meant for anyone who won't take it seriously and give it the respect it deserves.

There are deliciously selfish parts of a Dominant's role, but above all else are the needs of his submissive.

I'll soon be taking *selfish* pleasure from my doll's perfect pussy, but before I do, her body *needs* to be readied, or I could hurt her and ruin the trust between us that allows me to do whatever the fuck I want to her.

With the rolling tray table nearby and me back at her side, I transfer my phone there for easy access and open the brand-new bottle, this particular lube that doubles as a massage oil, and pour the liquid into my hand, setting it within reach for whenever I need more. I rub my palms together to warm the lubricant, knowing she detests when anything chilly touches her skin while she's naked. An example of something I can use as an actual punishment if need be.

My oiled hands go straight for her tits, and she sighs, melting into the padded table as I begin to massage the mounds that don't quite fill my big hands but are worthy of worship all the same. I take my time, squeezing and rubbing each breast before focusing on the hard peak in the center of one, then the other. Feeling her boobs is stimulating enough as it is, but watching her face contort with pleasure and then her hips as they start to subtly grind would be too much for a lesser man to handle.

My hands move lower, smearing the oil beneath her tits to her ribs, and I massage there, back up over her breasts, then down again, being careful not to inch too far toward her sides, where I know she's ticklish. Where some might find the feeling of being tickled fun and playful, my doll finds it irritating and torturous, and I avoid it as not to ruin her pleasure.

More punishment fodder for future use.

I squeeze more lube into my hand, warm it between my palms, and press them to her stomach, leaning over the table to slide them up her body evenly from this angle, then righting my arms so that I play her body as I would a piano. Up her left side and down the right, then back up the center between her breasts. And all the while, her hips work in an instinctive dance meant to coerce a mate into filling her up to bring her relief between those lovely thighs.

Thighs that give me a filthy idea for my first scene with no limits.

Quickly, I step over to the wall of various restraints and snatch off the wide Velcro cuffs adorned with silver D-rings, along with two adjustable straps with spring hooks on both ends. I'm by her side before the oil has even had a chance to cool on her skin, a prickle of sadistic pleasure running up my neck when I see her jump a little at the sudden sound of the Velcro pulling apart.

I loop it around the middle of her soft thigh, making sure it's tight but not enough to cut off circulation, and then clip one end of the strap to the D-ring I've positioned to be on the outside of her leg. I move around the foot of the table, then do the exact same thing to her right leg, tossing the other end of the strap under the table toward the head of it.

I circle back to where I began, pick up the silver spring hook off the floor that's attached to the strap leading to her left leg, and walk with it to the head of the playtable with a mischievous smirk taking over my entire face—as if it's a leash and her lush thigh is a pet being led somewhere to do something naughty.

Up until this moment, her legs have remained only slightly bent, just enough for me to encircle her limbs with the nylon cuffs. Now though, after squatting to take hold of her right leg's strap I tossed within reach a few seconds ago, I move back enough that I can watch with wicked delight as I begin to pull both ends toward me. With the straps together, hand over hand, I tug her legs up and back slowly, watching as her chest starts to move up and down with each breath getting deeper and faster. The farther I pull her legs back, the wider her bent knees spread apart, and I keep going until the stripes at the top of her high socks are at her armpits.

She whimpers at the utterly vulnerable position she's now in, and when I stand, my hand holding the straps down low to keep her where I want her, I lean over to ask in her ear, "Color?"

And for the first time tonight, she doesn't answer.

I move to look down into her face from above, asking again, "Color, doll?"

But again, no answer.

Her eyes are closed tightly, her breaths still coming quick and heavy, and before tonight, I would've immediately unhooked her wrists, headed to the other end of the playtable, unstrapped the Velcro from around her thighs, then pulled her into the safe cocoon of my arms. The scene would've ended right then, my painfully erect cock be damned. Not even the threat of a severe case of blue balls would've allowed me to continue playing with my sweet little doll while her fear instinct had her frozen.

But now, even with the loving and homicidally protective husband part of me raging just beneath the surface, it's the words in the birthday card she gave me tonight that are loudest in my mind. And it's my submissive's voice I hear them in.

I trust you with my body, mind, and soul even more than I trust my own instincts.

I trust you to push me past where my mind and fears tell me to stop.

I trust you to take my body's natural reaction to freeze the same way you would if a submissive called Yellow, not Red—pause to check in, assess what's going on, and then continue the way you see fit.

I trust in your judgement, to move past that boundary without going too far, but also to take me far enough I'll learn to conquer my mind's control over my body.

I want to be brave.

Decision made, I quickly attach the spring hooks to the metal loop beneath the table and adjust the straps so that they're taut.

I stand back up to my full height, fill my hand with oil that I heat up between my palms, then calmly, I reach over her to place one right in the center of her chest. I stare down into her face, her expression pained, but I know this position isn't physically hurting her. I could tell by the ease in which I pulled her legs back that her muscles aren't strained and her joints aren't aching. It's purely mental, or possibly partly emotional. This position is one of the most vulnerable, her most intimate parts not only totally exposed but spread open, and her hands being bound above her head means she has absolutely no way of covering herself. She's completely at my mercy.

"Doll, look at me," I order, my hand moving up and down from the power behind each of her breaths. When she doesn't do as I command, I get close to her ear and lower my voice to a purr. If she wants to be able to hear what I say, she'll have to take control of her breathing. It's the technique I've always used when she's frozen in fear, only it's the first time she's not swaddled in my lap with my entire body acting as the blanket.

"Breathe, my pretty toy. You're safe with me. Come out of your head and feel my hand on your heart. It's only me—the man you've entrusted to bring you pleasure. You know I'd never do anything to truly hurt you."

I see, hear, and feel her take a purposefully deeper breath before it stutters on its way back out.

"That's my strong girl. My brave little doll. Look at you. You make your Dom so fucking proud, my perfect sub. Do it again for me. Deep and slow," I murmur, and she does, this breath not as choppy on the exhale. "Good girl."

But as proud as I am that she's gaining control over this moment of fear, I don't want her to slip *all* the way back into the completely surrendered state she was in before quite yet. I needed her responsive now for what I have planned for the rest of our scene.

So instead of continuing to lull her with soft praise, I stand back up as she keeps working on smoothing out her breaths and move my hand from the center of her chest to massage her breast. I reach the other one farther down her body to rub up and down the inside of one lifted thigh, then switch and continue on with the relaxing but arousing manipulation.

When her breathing is back to normal, I look up to see her right foot make a circle in the air. A sign of discomfort she might not even realize she made. Without a word, I head to the opposite end of the table, my nostrils flaring as I force myself to focus on the task at hand instead of the incredible sight before me.

I undo the buckle of one chunky-heeled Mary Jane, then slip it off her pink-sock-covered foot, hearing her sigh. And it's no wonder—the shoe is heavy as shit. The pressure on her ankles with them weighing her feet down as they were forced to hover in the air would definitely be uncomfortable. I undo the other shoe, watching her face this time as I reverse the infamous Cinderella moment, yet her expression shows the same as the princess's when her foot slipped into her perfect-fitting glass slipper.

Pure relief.

"Better, pretty dolly?"

"Yes, Master," she says on an exhale, rolling her feet, and her ankles crack loudly.

I quirk an eyebrow as I watch for what I know is coming, smiling to myself when I see the blush steal across her cheeks.

Fuck, I love her.

I carry the heavy-ass shoes over to the trunk and set them on the floor in front of it, then return to the foot of the table. And I finally allow myself to take in the fantasy come to life that's bound before me.

Bent legs open wide and all the way back so that her knees

reach the outer sides of her breasts, the position is in stark contrast to the implied innocence of the pink socks that stretch from her pointed toes to where they now stop just above the bend. And farther up, the added visual of her arms stretched high above her head, bound together by black leather cuffs around those fragile little wrists…

"If only you could see yourself through my eyes, pretty toy. You'd never again worry that you're not enough," I say, reaching over to grab my phone and hoping she doesn't open her eyes before I have a chance to snap a photo. She looks utterly vulnerable but so at peace about that predicament, and the juxtaposition, the vision she makes, is something I don't think will ever be topped for the rest of my life. My flash off, I capture what will now be my most prized inanimate possession. I glance at the photo, seeing it's perfectly lit thanks to the auto adjust feature, and I already know I'll be printing it small enough for my wallet and large enough to fill an entire wall of our playroom at home.

"You'd see the fucking *dream* you are," I add, replacing my phone on the tray. With her arms attached to the head of the playtable and her bottom half pulled up, there's too much space between me and my sub's pussy for my liking. So, squatting to look beneath the table, I find the hinge releases, and like magic, the boundary between us disappears when that part of the table drops away. I stand back up and try to contain my rising sadistic giddiness as I refill my hand with lube.

I'm proud of my-damn-self when I manage not to go straight for her pussy that's right there for the taking. Instead, I stroke up and down her inner thighs, moving my hands to the outside of her legs to her hips and underneath to squeeze her ass. For long minutes, I treat her to a pampering massage that covers every inch of her skin I can reach in oil while she's bound this way—other than the small stretch of dark pink flesh right in the center of it all.

She's making those instinctive grinding motions again, begging me without words to touch where I've refused to graze even a finger this entire time I've had her on my table. Pitiful little whimpers fall from her lips, her face a mask of need so strong it borders on pain, and still, my oiled hands run up her belly, over her heaving tits, then down her sternum, only to cut to the sides right before I get to her mound to rub up her inner thighs.

It's not until a sob releases from her chest and out her mouth that I pretend that I just now noticed her desperation. "Aw… what is it, doll? You don't like your massage?"

"Yes, Master," she whines, and I smirk.

"Yes, you don't like your massage?"

"N-No, Master," she stutters, clearly unable to think straight enough to understand it's a trick question.

"*No,* you don't like your massage?"

"N-n—" She sucks in a breath as I come within an inch of where we both want me to touch, but my hand reverses once again. "I… I… I…."

"What's that, little toy? Your instructions don't say anything about a response beginning with 'I'. Maybe I should press the red button. Your card did say that I should push the emergency stop if something seems wrong."

"*No,* Master!" she begs forcefully, and I grin wickedly. Her eyes are clamped shut, but the expression takes over my face regardless. This is just too fucking sweet.

"Uh oh…" My hands stroke so close to her pussy I can feel the texture of the lube change slightly as it mixes with her natural wetness that's seeping from her slit. "I really think I might need to press that emergency stop. Your voice response is sounding rather bossy for a fuck doll meant only for me to use for my pleasure."

Her teeth snap shut and her jaw clenches at that, and I chuckle darkly. But when I pull my eyes from her face to look down at her pussy that's already much darker and swollen from how aroused she is without even being touched, I know I can't torture her any longer.

Finally, on the next downward stroke, I use my whole hand to glide over her center, and she jolts and cries out like she's been electrocuted. My movements never stopping, the heel of my palm presses harder on the upstroke, and I watch fascinated as her spread slit clenches when her clit gets attention.

I repeat the move with my flattened hand over and over again, my fingers pressed tightly together to make one smooth surface as I run it over her pubic bone, down her slit, then back up. I'm careful not to get too close to her asshole, because I don't want to risk giving her an infection by mixing things that should never be mixed inside a sweet little pussy. A fact that a disturbing number of men *and women* don't know. If I decide to add anal play to the festivities, it will be done with something—a finger or a toy—that won't go anywhere near her slit after it touches her tightest hole.

Her hips are gyrating against my hand, trying to ride it even as the straps won't allow her to. She's panting ferociously with her arousal, and I swear I've never seen her more turned on and needy. It's fucking intoxicating.

My next strokes are done with both oily hands, the pressure concentrated on her outer lips, then move more toward the center to massage between her inner and outer labia. She cries out in pleasure, and I glance up her body, realizing I was staring, mesmerized, my mouth damn near hanging open as I watched her pussy take on different shapes while I gave her a yoni massage I only ever dreamed about.

Not because I didn't want to before now, but because my little doll would've been mortified by the idea of being so utterly exposed.

"Yellow, Master," she suddenly calls out, and my eyes shoot to her face as she tilts her head up to look down her body at me, my motions stopping but my hands remaining on her pussy.

"What is it, doll? Fuck the role playing. Tell your Master what you need," I order, taking in her expression, which looks like she's about to burst into tears.

"Please, Seven. I can't take any more. It… hurts I need you so badly. Please."

The last word comes out on a sob, and I swear to God, it would've been my undoing if she hadn't given me that card.

Instead, keeping my eyes locked on hers as she begs me with them down the length of her body, I only slip one finger inside her sopping heat.

Her eyes roll back in relief for only a second before they change, growing wide with worry and in their depths as she realizes I'm not going to give her exactly what I know she'd been begging for. I pull the one finger out before gently sliding it back into her tight channel, a sweet kind of torture when she needs something thick and more stimulating to soothe the ache inside her. I feel her muscles clamp around it, trying to seek pleasure from the single digit.

This would've been actual torture for *me* just yesterday, when the sadist in me was still muzzled and kenneled, seeing my girl so anguished. But now that he's been set free and even encouraged to play, it's nothing but glee that I feel as her desperation grows.

It's not until she starts to chant, "Please... please... please... please... please, Master... *please,*" that I finally slip in a second finger, and she lets out a moan sexier than any porn star's in existence, and there's no denying that it's one hundred percent real.

I pull my fingers out, and instead of thrusting them right back in, I spread them into a V and run them up between her pillowy pussy lips and dark folds, circling her clit at the top before backtracking. And then I finally thrust back inside. With my other hand, I add even more stimulation by pulling back the hood over her hard little nub, and I repeat the path I made before, hearing her precious moan in response.

I do this over and over and over again, creating a rhythm she catches onto, anticipating each time I'm going to insert them inside her juicy core, because she now tilts her hips as much as she can on every plunge to meet them, in an attempt to create more friction.

But the next time I pull them out, stroke up her lips, circle her exposed little clit, then make my descent, her naughty little trick gets her in trouble, because it's not two but three of my thick fingers that she shoves herself down on.

Her head flies up from the table, her mouth an O of silent surprise, her breath ceasing to exist. Even though she is slippery as fuck with lube and her own wetness, three of my flattened fingers is a lot for her tight little pussy. It's not the girth, since my cock is much more filling than my middle three digits, but the shape and angle as I slide them inside that feels so different. I keep my fingers side by side and stroke them along the top of her channel, and her thighs quiver at the direct contact with her G-spot.

She's still holding her breath as she stares at our connection, and like flicking a switch inside her, I make a "come here" motion with all three fingers, and she gasps, then calls out, "Oh… God! Thank you, Master!"

The unrestrained volume from my normally soft-spoken sub and the words she released send my hips forward in a thrust that's purely instinctual, as I made no conscious effort to hump the air like a dog in heat. And the involuntary reaction that once would've pissed me off, as it was a show of lack of control, has the opposite effect with my little doll. It makes me horny as fuck. It makes me fucking proud. Her newfound confidence, of not giving a fuck, so sexy it made even *me*—a Dom with the highest level of self-control—loosen my grip on the reins. My girl letting go of her shyness and restraint and allowing her body to do whatever it wants.

Well, as much as it can while bound and at my mercy.

I do it all over again, pulling out, smoothing up her folds, circling her swollen clit, running down her slit, thrusting in along the top wall, then adding that extra-special stroke on the way back out to start the pattern all over again.

Once more, I get into the rhythm, my toy discovering that when she turns her hands inward, she can grasp the strap clipped to her wrist cuffs, and she can use it to pull her body up and release to fuck herself on my fingers on the intake. I allow it, since she hasn't been told to hold still and it doesn't disrupt what I'm doing to her. Plus, it's arousing as hell, watching my desperate girl try to find relief in any way she can.

She's never been edged like this before. I normally try to get her off as many times as physically possible, never denying her orgasms, since collecting hers gives me a sense of pride. But this?

This could be my new favorite pastime.

It's brought out a whole new side of her neither of us thought we'd ever meet.

Too needy to be embarrassed.

Too deliriously aroused to be self-conscious.

Too fraught with desire to worry about anything other than chasing a more intense pleasure.

She's so beautiful in this state that I now can't choose which turns me on more—my doll who flushes and cringes, or this uninhibited one.

Thankfully, I don't have to decide between one or the other.

Because this beautiful creature is *all mine.*

Watching her face, and just like before, I give her no warning the next time I enter her pussy, this time adding my pinky. But it's not the small addition of my little finger that makes her suck in a gasp of shock and then whine at the intrusion. It's the depth, which causes the knuckles along the top of my palm to slide in too.

Her eyes widen at the vulgarity of the scene between her legs, and she begins shaking her head and wiggling to dislodge my hand or get away. In a soft tone, I doubt she even realizes it when she starts to beg quickly, "No, no, no, no, no…," even as her pussy clenches around me with her movement. "*Nonononononono…*" her mouth is saying, but that's not the magic word to get me to stop, and her body is demanding me to do anything but quit when she starts to grind.

And then her head falls back to the padded table, pressing into it until her back arches, forcing her hips into an angle the gives her even more of my hand.

"Fuck yeah, my needy girl. Taking it all like a good little slut doll. Look at how much those pretty pussy lips stretch. And I can feel your cunt sucking on my fingers. Are you trying to pull even more inside?" I prompt, but she's back to the gloriously mindless state from earlier when I was feeding her mouth my cock, so I give her what her body is begging for.

I start to pump all four fingers in and out of her, gentle but faster, then use the thumb of my other hand to start rubbing her clit in incessant circles that makes the muscles of her inner thighs start to shake. That hand serves another purpose as well, holding her still as I press her to the table. As I speed up, any movement on her part could end up with me going in at an angle that would hurt, and the last thing I want to do in this moment is bring her out of this level of bliss I don't believe she's ever reached before.

Her mouth is open in the silent O once again as she holds her breath, seems to recognize she's doing it, so she releases the oxygen from her lungs quickly before sucking in more to hold… over and over, until…

"Master…?" Her voice is music. A cross between confusion, not understanding the new intensity of sensations, and a plea—for more, for permission, for everything I'll allow her to feel.

"Yes, pretty toy. You can come. Give it to your user, the one who owns you," I growl, my left hand pressing her steady, my thumb making constant circles on her clit, and my entire right hand sans my thumb disappearing over and over into her little pussy as I watch with rapt attention.

Her labia are stretched obscenely. Her entire center from mound to tailbone and hip to hip is drenched in lube and her own juices, shiny and downright delicious-looking beneath the playroom lights. And when she screams just as I feel her walls start to milk my hand, I tilt it at an angle while I keep pistoning, my fingertips pressing up toward her stomach and my knuckles to her perineum. And like I know will happen but she's never experienced, a geyser of her wetness shoots out of her pussy and splashes up my whole arm and across my abs.

"*Fuck* yeah!" I whisper to myself, feeling like the king of the fucking world, my queen blessing me with her own holy water.

"Oh… *God*!" she cries, and another stream of liquid erupts on a second wave of her orgasm.

Each time her pussy pulses while she continues to come, she squirts, the release and relief and the pleasure prolonging the monumental event.

And before those pulses have a chance to wane, I pull my hand out of her cunt and grip her thighs. I yank her back down to the very end of the table from where her tugs on her wrist restraints moved her upward, and while her pussy is fluttering like it's trying to suck the cum right out of a cock, I line up my dick and bury myself to the hilt in one thrust.

"Fuck!" she screams, a word rarely used by my doll, which makes it hit different, and it's like NOS to my system, my speed and roughness picking up as I pump my hips.

An endless string of nonsensical murmured words come from the head of the table as I fuck her at a punishing pace, the flutters inside her gripping heat never-ending while she completely surrenders.

But as primal as I've gone in the last few minutes, I remain zeroed-in on my submissive's every behavior and her safety. Her mind may have given over completely to her pleasure, but I know she shouldn't remain bound this way for much longer, or her joints will ache for days. And I'd rather use up her pain tolerance in much more adventurous ways during that time.

As I keep up my thrusts to the tune of her sweet nothings, I easily release the Velcro around her thighs, hearing her groan of relief as her legs come down to frame my hips. I lean forward and brace myself on one arm, still fucking into her as I reach and release the spring hook clipped to her cuffs. And then I put both elbows to the table to encircle each of her shoulders with one of my hands, squeezing and massaging them for a minute before taking hold of her linked wrists, pulling them with me as I stand back up.

The contrast between the black leather cuffs and the baby-pink thigh-high socks makes too debaucherous a picture to ruin by freeing her completely, so they remain in their bindings as I take hold of her thighs, gripping her right where they meet her hips.

"Get ready, little doll. I'm about to test just how much my mindless fuck toy can take before danger of damaging Pleasure Sleeve 2 is detected," I quip, hearing a sound escape her that's between a giggle and a nervous "eep." And that's the last thing I say before I tighten my grip and use it as leverage to start giving her thrusts she's never felt before.

I don't jackhammer into her with abandon like some tool who relies merely on his size instead of learning how to use it to *really* make a woman feel good. Each surge forward is done with purpose, coming to a stop with a collision of our sexes that reverberates pleasure throughout both our systems, before I steal my cock from her needy cunt, then do it all over again. I get rougher and rougher with every stroke until I notice a hum filling the room, and it's not until my lungs are painfully empty that I realize the sound was a growl coming from deep within my chest.

Yet again, she's so intoxicating I lost track of my own body and keeping it under rigid control. The primal part of me is the strongest it's ever been, my natural instincts wanting to take over our lovemaking, but it's my responsibility to keep my head on straight enough she won't get hurt, so I fight it back.

Until I look up from where my cock slides in and out of her now dark-red cunt and meet the pretty eyes filled with nothing but trust and love, and my little sub whispers, "Let go, Master."

CHAPTER 21

Twyla

"WHAT?" he growls, his hips faltering for only a single thrust before he returns to his precise pace.

I try to give him a reassuring smile, but the pleasure is too all-consuming to be able to focus on the muscles of my face. "Let go. Please, Seven. I want you to let loose on me."

He shakes his head, his sweat slinging and landing across my body. "No way, little toy. I don't want to break you."

My pussy clenches around his girth at the name he's called me tonight, and I hope it sticks around even after we're done with this sex doll game. "You won't, Master," I breathe, groaning as he hits an extra sweet spot inside me. "Please. I know you won't hurt me. You *can't*."

I don't say it like a challenge. I say it as a reminder that he is incapable of allowing himself to cause me harm.

He shakes his head again, but this time, there's less conviction in the gesture. He closes his eyes, seemingly trying to ignore me as his willpower falters. So I keep pressing.

"It's what I want from my Dom. Please, Seven. I want to see you let go the way *I* did while you fucked my mouth." My face flames as I say the last part, but it's worth it, because it has the effect I was hoping for. His hips thrust forward with extra power behind them. But I know he's got so much more he's holding back. I've always sensed it beneath the surface, and I don't want to be the reason he can't be himself and just let it out.

"You don't know what you're asking," he tells me, his voice going cold as he stares into my eyes with his beautiful hazel ones.

My nipples harden to a painful degree, finding the sadistic part of him he locked away from me so freaking sexy each time I catch a glimpse of it.

"I do," I assure him. "Please. It's what I want. Let go and show me. Let me be brave for my Master."

And that's apparently the right combination of words to unlock his cage. Because with a growl that's not only sexy but scary in its ferocity, Seven rips himself away from me, takes hold of my hips, and flips me in one easy move. I hit the padded table with an "oof" as I land on my stomach, and before I can spread my legs and prepare to take him from behind, his knees clamp them shut. My feet don't reach the floor, since the table is set to be the right height for his long legs, so I have no leverage in any direction. My arms are trapped beneath me, still bound at the wrists, but the table is so cushioned it doesn't hurt. I'm just completely immobilized.

And at the mercy of my Dom I just begged to go feral on my ass.

The feel of his long, thick, and extremely hard erection entering me this way—with my legs pressed together, my hips at the exact height he needs—takes my breath away. I've never felt so full, not even when he had the whole damn palm of his hand in my vagina a while ago. The sight had been grotesque to my own eyes, but the way he was looking at the act, like it was the sexiest thing he'd ever seen, combined with the magical way he moved his fingers inside me, I found myself incapable of caring how it appeared to me, especially as my eyes rolled back and I couldn't see it anymore. And the orgasms it produced were unlike any I've ever felt before.

If the ease in which he slipped his cock inside me afterward was anything to go by, it had made me rather slippery, and I feel my face heat even now from getting so wet.

At least he seemed to like the little bit of extra slickness I produced.

Now though, I'm grateful for every milliliter of lubrication between us, because his dick feels like it's doubled in length and girth at this angle. He goes slow at first, making sure he's completely coated, even as his hands suddenly grip my ass roughly, his fingertips digging in to my cheeks so hard I know they'll leave little bruises. And for some reason, the thought excites me.

My sister and friends have always been so proud, showing off the various marks left on their flesh after scenes with their husbands. But Seven has always been so careful in the way he handles me, the way he's never forceful enough to leave more than a little red mark that disappears quickly, no evidence left of it by the time we're dressed again. I was never jealous of their "souvenirs." I honestly didn't get why they'd want to be struck or grabbed hard enough to bruise or even bleed.

But now...

I don't know what flipped the switch inside me...

But I *get* it.

And I *want* it.

As he paws my butt cheeks, kneading my flesh way more roughly than during the massage he treated me to earlier, my hips try to lift off the table, seemingly trying to seek more of his ministrations. I hear him growl again, and the sound sends a shiver down my spine that ends with me clenching around him.

"Fuck, little doll. You like being manhandled," he rumbles behind me, not a question, an observation. One that surprises the both of us. Because I really, really do.

"Yes, Master," I exhale, my heart starting to race with anticipation, because something within me senses I'm about to get exactly what I asked for, and then some.

And then it happens.

With a brutally tight grip on each of my hips, I feel Seven pull all the way out of me, and then he thrust back inside so swift and hard it feels like my brain sloshes inside my skull.

He does it again.

This time, I feel my teeth rattle, and my eyes roll back in my head.

Again.

And again.

And again.

And by the sixth thrust, I'm back to being that fully surrendered fuck toy, just taking everything he's willing to give, each stroke pulling me deeper and deeper into an ocean of mind-numbing bliss.

I could drown in it, and I would die happily.

And then I'm aware he's pistoning his hips faster than I've ever felt before, his right hand leaving my hip to grip the back of my neck, then moves to my shoulder to give him even more leverage to fuck me like a savage beast. Like he's breeding me. And I freaking *love* it.

"Color?" floats around in my head, and I don't know if it's a distant memory of some other time he asked me to check in, or if it's been freshly spoken in my ear. Either way, my response leaves me in a sigh.

"Green, Master."

If he hadn't just asked me, then the words would only serve to urge him on. And that is fine by me.

Somewhere along this floating journey, a voice whispers that this must be subspace. The way people always described it before, it sounded much like dissociation, but my husband had assured me it was a much more positive experience than that.

I had dissociated during my assault five years ago, and while you'd think your mind shutting down to protect itself during a traumatic event would be a good feeling, it was actually scary and traumatizing in itself, since at the time, it didn't feel like I'd ever come out of it, not even when I was safely back in Seth's arms.

This is nothing like that.

This is what movies make you think being drunk or high feels like before you ever try those things yourself and reality bursts your bubble.

This is like that one quick second between a happy dream and waking up, when you don't quite know what's real.

And as blissfully relaxed as it is, I also feel stronger and more powerful than I've ever felt before, like I'm invincible. Like no amount of pain could hurt me in this state. In fact, it's almost as if the more pain I'm given, the deeper into this level of consciousness I'd go. And it occurs to me that *this* is probably what masochists are seeking whenever they play. Yes, they get off on the pain itself, but the pain leads to this. The delicious in-between. That same relief you get when you scratch a mosquito bite so hard you draw blood, and even though it hurts, you keep scratching, because the relief is worth the pain.

And then I'm coming. I'm orgasming, my pussy spasming and rippling around my Master's relentless cock as he pounds into me. But it's not the usual earth-shattering explosion that hits all at once after a build-up of stimulation. It's completely different, like I'm living in that moment right between the detonation and the mushroom cloud, as if someone hit pause on the exact frame that only shows a cylinder of flames before there's any smoke.

Or that moment after a scream but before your next inhale.

And I'm not coming out of it.

Yet unlike when I dissociated, the thought of staying like this isn't scary. I don't want to struggle against it or fight my way back to the surface of cognition. I could live here forever, with my Master fucking me into literal oblivion, my only purpose in life to be the vessel he takes his pleasure from.

"Color?"

"Fuuck…"

"…fill you up until you can taste it…"

"…marks on you, don't you?"

"Brand you with…"

"Take it like a good…"

"Yeah…"

"…my pretty toy?"

"…slutty little pussy wants…"

My Master's filthy words are birds that fly diagonally through my consciousness, entering from the bottom, then exiting out the top, or dive-bombing from above and disappearing beneath.

But as his grip on my shoulder tightens and he loops his other arm around the front of my hips, my body seeming weightless as he pulls me on and off his cock while he fucks up into me, using me like the sex doll I aimed to be for him, I hear it loud and clear when he yanks me up to growl in my ear.

"Take it all."

With one last thrust that's violent enough to bruise my insides—and a weird part of me hopes it does—he comes with a roar that breaks my entire body out in chills. His grip on me is brutal as I feel jet after jet of hot cum coat my walls, feeling like a soothing balm on the pain I begged for.

CHAPTER 22

Seven

EVERY MUSCLE in my body is at its tension limit as I come deep inside my doll's fist-like pussy. If I were to flex a single fiber any harder, that piece of me would be shredded. And with the last pulse of my orgasm, all of that tension leaves me at once, making me feel faint.

If there wasn't that sliver of conscious control that remained intact while the rest of me went full-on beast mode, I would collapse to the ground and stay there for the rest of the night. In fact, that still sounds like a great option, except I'll make sure to cushion my sweet submissive's landing when we fall.

I let her down my body until her front rests on the padded table once again, and when I ease out of her and take a step back, I can't help but notice she looks more like a sex doll now than she did while playing the role.

I gather her into my arms, and carry her over to the overstuffed leather chair against the wall we always use for aftercare. Once she's nestled just right in my lap so that she won't slip downward or fall over, I undo the cuffs that were stuck between her body and the playtable while I ravaged her, looking over that part of her I've always found so delicate and fragile. Her wrists are so petite they look as if they could be snapped between my fingers like a pencil. I'm happy to find them still intact.

I take one of her hands and lift it to my lips, my eyes meeting hers that are stuck at half-mast. If it weren't for the tiny permasmile on her face, I'd be a little worried. I watch her watching me as I kiss around her wrist, her gaze never leaving my mouth as I gently set that hand down and trade it for the other. I treat it to the same kiss-and-make-it-better as the first, seeing the corners of her lips lift a teensy bit higher when I place her palm against my bearded cheek and lock it there with my own.

I clear my throat that's suddenly clogged, telling myself to pull it together. Aftercare is an important part of our D/s dynamic. Some submissives don't want anything to do with it, but my little doll needs it to feel complete, and she soaks up every second of it like it fills something inside her, a bucket of love or worth or happiness that gets used up during daily life and has to be replenished frequently to keep her going. And I'm all too happy to give her free refills at every opportunity.

Tonight though, I want to use this opportunity to set things right *outside* our dynamic. Yes, it's manipulative, but when it comes to my wife, it's the only time her mind is at ease enough to not overthink the things I'm saying. And I need all the help I can get.

I huff out a single, quiet laugh, shaking my head a little, keeping our hands right where they are against my cheek. "I'm trying to think of anything… anything at all to say that could express to you...." I shrug, swallowing hard. "There are no words to articulate the praise you deserve, Twyla."

Her eyes open fully and blink at my use of her real name. When we're within the walls of the club, she's my doll, and I'm Master to her and Seven to everyone else. But I want her to know I'm not just speaking to her as my submissive. I'm talking to my wife, the mother of my child, my soul mate.

"Once I have a chance to process everything in your card and everything you did to prepare for the gift you gave me tonight, and the excellent execution of it"—I grin—"I'm sure I'll be able to wax poetic about all the ways you deserve the goldest of stars. But..." I shake my head again, saying softly, "Just... thank you."

I put every ounce of emotion I feel into those two simple words. And the way her eyes tear up, I know she feels it as she nods.

"You're welcome," she whispers.

I turn my face to kiss the center of her palm, then let it go to gather her closer to my chest. She presses it over my heart, where she starts to pet my chest hair like she does every chance she gets. Like *I'm* her personal security blanket or stuffy she uses to soothe herself. And it's one of my favorite roles in life—being the thing that brings her easy and immediate comfort.

"Things are going to change after tonight, my doll," I tell her, skimming my palm from her knee, down the outside of her thigh, up her hip and back, then back down again. I do this slowly over and over, knowing her shivers will start soon. Even after the lightest of play, adrenaline is always in abundance within my little sub because of her hair-trigger fear response. And once she starts to come down after that rush, she gets the shakes like she's just taken an ice bath each and every time. It's my job to keep her warm and comfort her through it until it passes.

"I want you to know I finally heard what you've been trying to tell me for years. Like, truly *heard* and *absorbed* your words and the unspoken ones between them."

She tilts her head back to look up at me with confusion in her eyes. "What are you talking about?" she whispers.

I tuck her face into its spot in the crook of my neck and shoulder. The shame I felt earlier is still inside me, and it feels like I can get what I have to say out a little easier if I don't have to say it to her face. It's cowardly, sure, but really, I know if I look into her eyes, I'll only see them fill with misplaced guilt, because my wife is a truly selfless woman who lives and breathes to take care of her family. And I'm making it my job to get her to see she deserves to be the person she is inside and doesn't need to alter herself to fit alongside anyone else.

"It's taken me this long to see that you've been losing parts of yourself to make everyone else happy. You've been cutting off little bits and pieces to make yourself fit inside the spot where you think each one of us needs you. And that stops now." My voice leaves no room for argument, but I continue to rub along her flesh, and like clockwork, her trembles begin.

"You gave up all parts of your adolescence and young adulthood as you focused solely on working toward your career. It was the one thing you wanted in life, and baby, you did it. But then you gave that up, because your sister needed you. You should feel no regrets about that, and I know you don't. I'm just saying it happened. You did give up your career, which at that time was the biggest part of *you*." My hand stops rubbing up her back long enough to squeeze her in order to emphasize the last word, and then it continues along its circuit.

"When you got here in town, there weren't any jobs available that would put that brilliant mind of yours to work doing what you loved, but instead of letting it get you down, you took the one position offered to you, even though it was the furthest thing outside your wheelhouse and comfort zone possible. Again, you gave up feeling confident and secure, because it was necessary in order for your sister and you to survive.

"And when you became the mother of my child, and our Luna girl started growing into the strong-willed miniature adult she already is at four years old, you gave up more parts of yourself so that I could be the dad *I* wanted to be. I wanted to be the hero, the good cop, the one she looks at like I hung the moon and can do no wrong. I wanted a Daddy's girl, a mini version of my wife, who looks at me with hearts in her eyes too. What I didn't realize was you can't give your little one every single thing they want, then expect them to grow up to be a well-rounded adult equipped with the knowledge and strength it takes to survive this world."

I swallow again, trying to find the right words to say all this so that she won't feel the need to make *me* feel better for doing *her* wrong. Because that's just who she is as a person and part of the reason I've always felt this overwhelming need to protect her at all costs. She's the type of person who's an easy target, who stands out like there's a neon arrow above her head pointing down at her to narcissists and manipulators and people with ulterior motives who prey on innocents like her.

"But *you* did. You knew all that long before it occurred to me just this evening. *Because* you have that ridiculously intelligent mind and *because* you yourself had to do whatever it took to survive. Everything you had to give up, and then everything you went through after you did, that all prepared you to become the parent who is actually doing their job *correctly*. Even though there's nothing about you that would earn you the title of 'bad cop,' you took on the role anyway, because it's what our daughter needs in order to take on the world when it comes time for her to. You took on that role, because you saw I didn't want to. That I wanted to be the fun one, the playful one, the one who makes her nothing but happy and spoils her rotten. You were *forced* to take on that role, because I refused to. And that's just not fucking fair."

I hear her sniffle when I stop the rush of words now pouring out of me, and then I feel the wetness streaming down my chest and abs. But instead of pulling her head back to look into her eyes as she cries, I get out what this was all leading up to, leaving no space for her to try to lighten my load as I shoulder my fuck-up and do what it takes to make it right.

"And like I said a minute ago, it stops now. From now on, our partnership as parents isn't good cop and bad cop. We are a united front. We have each other's back. We make decisions together, and that's that. I mean, come on. It's the only way the two of us are going to survive *Luna*. It'll take the two of us to face just one of her when she really puts her mind to something we don't want her to do. Hell, she figured out the 'go ask Daddy when Mommy says no' trick when she was only two. And when she couldn't get away with that any longer, she figured out the 'just wait until Daddy gets home and ask him first' trick. So… at least I taught her how to have a little patience, I guess."

That earns a giggle from my doll, whose shivers have finally subsided and tears seem to have stopped. I knew if I could just get to this part, the part where she'd realize she *wants* to split the burden of growing a future contributing member of society, that her need to keep my fragile male ego intact would give way to make a little room for her own happiness.

"But luckily, we've got a really great kid. Like... she's so fucking cool. And smart. And the imagination on that girl...." My voice is wistful, because I can't believe I helped make such an extraordinary little human. "And thanks to you taking on that role of disciplinarian as soon as you saw I wasn't going to step in and do it, it's more *upkeep* than starting with a hellchild who's never heard the word no." I chuckle, hugging my wife closer but finally letting go of the headlock I've had her in against my neck. She fully relaxes against me and tilts her head back to look up into my eyes.

"So, my lovely Twyla, my darling wife, my good little doll, and—your latest addition—my mindless, slutty fuck toy..." She blushes immediately, and I sigh in contentment. "I'm so glad I didn't fuck that out of you. Mm. What was I saying? Oh yeah. Repeat after me." I wait for her nod, and when I get it, I say in a threatening tone, "You just wait until Daddy gets home."

Her lips fold in so she can clamp them with her teeth, but her eyes give it away that she's trying not to laugh. I lift a brow in mock offense.

"What? You don't think I could punish Luna if she did something bad?"

She giggles softly. "Oh, I'm sure you could come up with something creative as a disciplinary action if need be. You're very good at that."

Ego stroked, I ask her, "Then why are you trying not to laugh?"

She grins. "Because you think *Luna* would ever take 'just wait until Daddy gets home' as a *threat*."

I burst out laughing, a belly laugh that's cathartic and makes most of the shame I felt at dinner dial back to a level that's no longer overstimulating. When I get it all out, I sigh. "Yeeeah, you're probably right. It's definitely something we'd have to work on. But until then, I want you to practice. I know there are things that will happen while I'm at work, and you'll need to take action right then. But when she's *really* being a turd, instead of getting overwhelmed from trying to take it all on yourself, I demand that you wait. You wait and let Daddy step in. Got it?"

She bites her bottom lip, her eyebrow lifting. "I just clenched."

Both my brows shoot up. "Oh yeah? Was it the command at the end or the 'Daddy'?"

She smiles sweetly, then snuggles into her nook, her hand starting up its petting of my furry chest once again. "It was the part where I'm going to get to be the kind of mom I've always dreamed of being."

I swallow thickly, fighting off the tinge of guilt her words dig up. I can't change the past, but I can spend the rest of our childrearing years doing it the *right* way.

I chuckle after a moment of just holding her close, and she looks up at me. "What is it?"

I smile wickedly. "Ever looked into the '50s household lifestyle?"

She shakes her head.

"Wife's a homemaker, takes care of the kids, cooks, cleans—the stereotype."

She snorts. "So what I do anyway when I'm not at the store?"

I poke her ribs, and she jumps. "Right. But they mastered the art of 'just wait until your father gets home,'" I tease, and then get to what I was really talking about. "And if it's a 24/7 dynamic with kinky fuckery added to the mix, think of all the possibilities."

She does. She spends a moment thinking about what just those few little breadcrumbs could lead to, and then she nods. "If it's anything like what I'm imagining, then I'd definitely be interested. Those cute housewife dresses… frilly aprons… those feather dusters that do nothing but toss the dust into the air for you to breathe or land somewhere else. A fairytale version of *Madmen*… without all the drugs and cheating."

I wrap my arms tightly around her and—not giving a flying fuck that the Seven part of me wouldn't be caught dead doing such a thing—I shimmy us giddily a la Cam from *Modern Family*. "Daddy's goin' shopping!"

The End

For the Reader & Acknowledgments

I hadn't written a book in over a year and a half. 2023 was just too wild in my little family to form a complete thought, much less a whole-ass book.

In March 2023, we adopted my goofball, adorable seventeen-year-old nephew, Bret, to give him a fresh start in Texas, much like my big brothers did for me in college. (Read all about the entire experience in *The Blogger Diaries Trilogy*, the true story of how I met my husband of—at the time of this publication—fourteen years.) Bret lived in my Podunk hometown in NC, and he dropped out of high school during Covid, because... hell, I would've too. That shit sucked for all of us, especially the kids.

After we got him settled (turning my library into a boy cave —*sobs) the next step was teaching him ways to overcome his lifelong debilitating social anxiety. Podunk hometown, remember? It doesn't have the best options for mental healthcare, hence why I didn't even get diagnosed with all my neurospiciness until I was in my mid-twenties. And with the ADHD and "touch of the 'tism" as my family lovingly likes to call what most of us inherited, that was no small feat.

But Bret was lucky enough to go from being basically an only child (his big sis is much older and moved out when he was wittle) to suddenly thrown into the Robichaux mix, gaining THREE younger siblings (15, 13, and 3 at the time) plus an aunt and uncle who didn't just let him hide from the world. Soon enough, he went from being unable to order his own food at a drive-thru, to being *everyone's* favorite server at a nursing home —his very first job. The perfect job for him, really, because he's so stinkin' handsome and genuinely sweet, and those little old ladies just ate him up.

In a "pinch his cheeks" way, not a weird cougar way.

The cheeks on his face, I mean… not his—

Yeah. You get me.

All the residents were so kind to him, and they were just what he needed to go from unable to make words come out of his mouth when he got nervous, to coming home and telling us what a good day he had, stories they told him, and adventures in the kitchen. He did so well they even started teaching him to cook, which he really enjoyed. Another bonus lesson, since he could barely make ramen when he first moved in with us lol! (I really can't blame him for this though, since his mama is such a damn good cook. I would've let her spoil me rotten too. Love you, Nay.)

Anyhoo.

Over the next several months, Bret did Driver's Ed and got his license, earned his GED, and—after lots of thinking and conversations with Uncles Jason, Logan, Mark, and Tony, plus his dad—he enlisted in the US Army. He recently graduated bootcamp and is currently in AIT, and we couldn't be prouder.

On top of all that, and besides all the craziness that comes with having two teenage girls and a preschooler, I decided to hop in my car here in Texas in June '23 and drive nonstop to kidnap my mom from aforementioned Podunk town in NC. A little birdy (my Uncle Sam, Mom's younger brother) called to tattle that Mom wasn't taking very good care of herself, and that just wouldn't do.

My dad passed away a few years ago, so it's just her in our big-ass childhood home, and with no one else to cook for, my mother—with all sorts of cardio and kidney conditions—thought it wise to live on fast-food hot dogs and microwaveable meals.

Ya know… the ones with like a gajillion grams of sodium? (*facepalm)

So yeah, I threw Avary and Vivian into my Bronco while Bret and Josalyn held down the fort, and we road-tripped it across the country, not even telling MomMom we were coming.

The best part was letting Vivi ring her doorbell while Avary and I hid. So when she answered the door, it was just her four-year-old grandbaby who lives in Texas, standing there like she decided to go visit her MomMom by herself. It was great.

We gave her no choice.

You don't like to fly? No problem! Your chariot awaits.

You can't ride that far straight-through like we do? Say less. I've already promised Avary we'll make lots of stops to see cool shit on the way back home, so we can make the trip in a few days instead of all at once.

No excuses, woman.

And it ended up being the best little spontaneous week we've ever had, which the girls still talk about daily. The Atlanta Botanical Gardens, the Tuskegee Airmen Memorial, and New Orleans to top it off. But the best stop by far was when I asked Mom if there was anything she'd like to see; I didn't care how far off the path it was. She thought about it and asked for me to look up how far we were from her favorite YouTuber's shop, and it turned out we were less than an hour away.

Maymay Made It, here we come!

The entire way, she was so excited. This was her scrapbook-making QUEEN. She kept saying over and over how thrilled she would be if she was actually there for her to meet. But if she wasn't, then she'd be excited to meet her assistants too. Mom even knew all their names and told me how much she loved Maymay's husband, who ends all the YouTube videos with Bible verses and uplifting prayers.

We were HYPED.

We pulled into the shop's parking lot, and I've never seen my mom get out of a car so fast in all my life. Her seventy-six-year-old ass MOVED. We walked inside and were met by one of the assistants, and Mom recognized her immediately, greeting her by name.

But unfortunately, Maymay wasn't in that day. Her hubby had a doctor's appointment, and then they had Vacation Bible School that evening, so they took the day off.

We were all a little bummed, but thankfully, Mom was just excited to be able to shop in Maymay's store. She'd been following her videos for years and had recreated so many of the scrapbooking pages and papercrafts she learned from them, so just being in her idol's space was good enough for her.

We told the assistant our story, how we were from Texas, but we went and kidnapped Mom from NC and were on our way back, and how this was the one stop she wanted to make along the way. Mom even told her a story that got me choked up, about how after my dad passed away, she'd watch Maymay's videos in bed at night, her husband's scriptures at the end soothing her enough to finally fall asleep by herself thanks to his comforting voice.

While Mom was in a frenzy, scouring every shelf and rack

and filling her basket with all the sheets of paper, stamps, glue, stickers, and pens she could possibly ever need in a lifetime, I noticed the assistant hurry out the front door.

That's suspicious.

I had never seen Mom's show before, so I didn't know what Maymay looked like, but…

My spidey senses were telling me something big was about to happen.

So I got my phone out and hit record when I saw the assistant coming back inside with a man and woman who had pulled up next to my car. Just in case.

"Ma'am?" the young woman called for my mom.

And when Mom turned around and saw her standing there with the couple just inside the door—omg, I'm tearing up remembering this—her mouth dropped open, and I swear her knees buckled for a moment before she took off toward them.

She didn't even say a word, and Maymay didn't miss a beat, as my sweet, tiny little mama walked right up to her and wrapped her in the biggest hug like they were long-lost friends. When she finally pulled back, all the words she couldn't get out before started falling out all at once—nervous fangirling, listing all the projects she'd done from her videos, how pretty she always thought she was but she's even prettier in person…. And Maymay was the most gracious sweetheart throughout the whole visit.

It turns out they got done with her husband's doctor appointment and just stopped by to switch vehicles on their way to VBS, but her assistant told her that her biggest fan was on a road trip and that her shop was her number-one stop. So they came inside just so they could meet my mom.

We also told them what my mom said about falling asleep to

their videos and how much she appreciated the prayers at the end of each one, and Maymay's hubby told her that meant the world to him—since he figured a lot of people just skip that part—and gave her the best hug.

So if you're ever passing through or close to Clanton, Alabama, you should definitely stop by Maymay Made It. You'll never meet a kinder group of people, who absolutely made my mama's whole year.

And worth getting kidnapped.

Mom has been living with us since we abducted her one year ago last week. We still let her have her beloved hot dogs every once in a while, but mostly she's spoiled with her son-in-love's delicious cooking. Eventually, I know we have to let our hostage go so she can spend time at home in NC, but I've managed to keep her here with various doctor's appointments spaced out just enough she can't leave. She's currently healing from kidney stones being lasered, but since it's hotter than Hades here in Houston right now, I guess I'll let her go as soon as the stints come out…

But only for a couple of months.

Then I'll be dragging her ass right back to Texas.

So, all this to say… a bish has been busy.

But if you read all that, you might have noticed a few things from my past year-and-a-half break from writing made it into this book.

I learned what washi tape is at Maymay Made It.

The research I did for Bret's anxiety inspired a lot of the things Twyla went through, like freezing and being unable to speak.

Plus a lot of things I learned at the BDSM author event I was blessed to be a part of in September, the Smut Lovers Convention.

Which led to me finding—and hubby and I becoming a part of—a local kink group that have quickly become friends I know we'll have forever. I have never felt more accepted or had as much fun in my entire life than I do now, being a part of HAKIE SACK—Houston Area Kinksters Incorporating Entertainment, Socializing, Arts, Community & Kinship.

To have this awesome and eclectic group of likeminded people to just do fun, completely innocent shit with, like mini golf, trying different local breweries, or meet-ups for each other's birthdays, has made a world of difference in this introverted little author's mental health. And to be part of a strictly vetted, trustworthy group to experience not-as-innocent shit with, like "BDSM buffet parties," where members who specialize in certain acts or tools give people who have always wanted to try something the chance to safely get a taste of those things to see if they like it or not, has been inspiring for my work and incredibly eye opening when it comes to self-discovery.

Here's where I'd like to insert something I learned at the convention that I've come to realize a lot of people who read BDSM romance don't know either.

BDSM and sex are two completely separate entities.

Because most romance readers' knowledge of the kink community comes from fictional love stories, they don't realize that people who practice BDSM do not always incorporate anything to do with sex or genitalia whatsoever. There are D/s relationships between people who have never once touched each other's no-no zones. The sub can go to their Dom to consensually get the shit beaten out of them, or what have you, and that's the extent of their scene—no kissing, no nothing.

That blew my mind when that was clarified for me by the incredible teachers at The Woodshed in Orlando.

That same conversation is where I also learned that some Doms do not give aftercare to their sub but instead hand the sub over to their "person" once their scene is complete. I included this little tidbit in this book, when I talked about Seven in the past only playing with subs who had a Dom of their own to handle aftercare. It's something I'd never read in a BDSM romance before, so I made sure to do my thing and include it, since I love teaching things throughout my stories.

BDSM relationships are completely customizable, and through strong, honest communication and negotiating what each person wants and needs / doesn't want or need, every partnership is 100% different. And an even cooler aspect about a D/s relationship is the fact that it is ever evolving within itself. This is what I wanted to portray with Seth and Twyla's new story.

One might begin a relationship in a certain role, like maybe as a service sub with a low pain tolerance. But time passes, and that sub might see a friend experiencing pure bliss as they're being flogged, and it sparks an interest to see what the big deal is. So they try a super-soft flogger made out of fluffy yarn, and that feels good, so they try one made out of wide, brushed leather, and that feels even better… and then the next thing you know, she's got a whole-ass collection of impact toys that she can't get enough of.

That's what happened to Jason and me for sure.

We have been blessed with the best mentors we could've possibly been lucky enough to land. Tracy and Monte are like our Mama and Daddy when it comes to our journey in this community, and I can't even imagine there being better leaders-turned-friends.

While we don't do anything sexual with anyone else—100% monogamous, because y'all know I'm homicidal-level possessive, and he loves it—we're able to learn things by "playing" with our mentors. Well… I do. He just likes to watch and then take advantage of me (lol).

For example, Monte is a rigger. (Remember your lesson from this book? He does the rope tying.) He didn't have much of an interest in rope until Tracy discovered a passion for being tied and suspended. That's when they started going to rope bondage classes, so he could provide that for her, and now he's a rigging BADASS. He calls himself a service top, because he gains all his good feelings from making others happy by being a safe and trustworthy person they can go to, who can provide what they'd like to experience with no worries.

So, I've had an absolute blast getting to try all sorts of shibari and suspensions, because my mentor loves to do that for people without anything sexual having to do with it. Monte rigs me up, while Jason watches—and fucks with me while I'm helpless lol—then when I'm back on the ground and untied, I get the best Papa-Bear hug from Monte as I thank him for all his hard work and time. The scene always ends with a sincere "you're welcome" and a reminder that he got just as much out of it as I did—because he's 100% a Daddy Dom, knows how Littles tend to feel like a burden, and is always quick to shut that shit down.

Okay, I totally squirreled and went off on a tangent there. What was I saying?

Oh yeah, D/s relationships are not only customizable but also ever evolving. And that's what I wanted this book to show, even though it was a little more dramatic than how it happens in real life. But that's just part of the fun of fiction. In real life, it can happen way more casually, slowly over time, as things are added or taken away bit by bit while each person discovers new things they like or dislike. There were things on my soft limits list that are now some of my very favorite treats. There are things that were once on my *hard* limits list that we now occasionally dabble in when I'm feeling extra adventurous. And you know what? There's nothing to say we can't do that.

You ain't gonna get in trouble for growing.

As long as it's consensual, let your freak flag fly.

So, moving on to the acknowledgments part of this backmatter…

Let's see, I've covered HAKIE SACK, Smut Lovers, The Woodshed, Monte and Tracy…

Oh! Tracy. I haven't given her the thanks she deserves.

Tracy, you are one of a kind in a way that is not the overused term of endearment. I've literally never met anyone like you, so selfless and loving and accepting and genuinely kind for no reason other than you're just a good fucking human. Thank you for continuing to invite us to things, when at first it was super-hard to get Jason to leave the house for anything outside a 2-mile radius that wouldn't take longer than ten minutes. You never got discouraged or gave up on us, and thanks to that, all I have to do now is ask him if we can go out to play with our friends, and he only says no if there's a really good reason. I've learned so much about the community and about myself ever since you welcomed me with open arms, and I'm so blessed to have you as not only my mentor but my friend.

And thank you for our writing sleepover! Your presence and talking through what I wanted the doll remote to do got me past a block I thought would surely end up with me not writing for another year. I can't wait to read the book that'll include all those words you were able to write that night, and for the many meetups, events, parties, thrifting dates, and writing sleepovers to come!

Speaking of parties: Thank you, Bunny, for the invite to your birthday party. It was the perfect motivation to finish my book on time. What better reward for completing a book about a Dom and his sub playing at a BDSM club for his birthday, than this sub and her Dom getting to go to a BDSM club for our friend's birthday!

Thank you, Shannon, for our writing dates when I wrote the first half of this book at the beginning of the year. I started out just trying to write a fun, short little Valentine's Day novella using one of my readers' favorite couples in order to get back into it after not writing for so long. When I told you my characters were talking too much and it didn't seem like everything was going to fit into a novella, nor was I going to be done in time for Valentine's Day, you encouraged me to just say fuck it and keep writing until I was happy with my book. I'm so glad I didn't try to rush or shut up the voices in my head, because now Seven has a sequel that actually turned out being longer than his original story! LOL!

Thank you to my Alpha girls, Christi, Crystal, Vanessa, and Stacia. Y'all are the best hype girls I could ever ask for, who also give it to me straight if something sucks. I love y'all for that. And thank you to Barb, my amazing editor, and Casey, my hawk-eyed proofreader, for fixing things even my OCD-diagnosed ass missed and for your notes that bring me joy.

Thank you to my mommy and big girls for entertaining Vivi when both Jason and I needed to work, and for being understanding and not making me feel guilty for having to hide away to get it all done. I love y'all so much, and it was a huge reminder to cherish every second I do get to spend with my family.

Most of all, thank you to Jason, my hubby, my DD, my soulmate, my everything. I couldn't have done this without you. Literally. You kept the kids, Mom, and me alive while I used all my physical and mental energy to write. You brought me food and coffee every single time I asked, and lots of times when I forgot to ask, without a single word of complaint. You are the man of my dreams, the Dom of my imagination brought to life, and words can't express how truly happy I am in the life we share. I love you, Daddy!

Finally, thank you to my readers, whose excitement over not only Seth getting a new story but the fact that I was writing ANYTHING was the best motivation for putting the work in I could possibly ask for. I'm relieved to be able to give this to you, and I hope you love it as much as you anticipated reading it. If it weren't for those of you who tell me how much these books mean to you, then I would lose this part of me, because I don't do much for just myself. So thank you for your continued comments, posts, messages, and emails, so I have an excuse to indulge and give life to the voices in my head.

Made in the USA
Las Vegas, NV
18 July 2024

92490703R00133